PENGUIN CLASSICS

The Shadow Puppet

'I love reading Simenon. He makes me think of Chekhov'
– William Faulkner

'A truly wonderful writer . . . marvellously readable – lucid, simple, absolutely in tune with the world he creates'
– Muriel Spark

'Few writers have ever conveyed with such a sure touch, the bleakness of human life'
– A. N. Wilson

'One of the greatest writers of the twentieth century . . . Simenon was unequalled at making us look inside, though the ability was masked by his brilliance at absorbing us obsessively in his stories'
– *Guardian*

'A novelist who entered his fictional world as if he were part of it'
– Peter Ackroyd

'The greatest of all, the most genuine novelist we have had in literature'
– André Gide

'Superb . . . The most addictive of writers . . . A unique teller of tales'
– *Observer*

'The mysteries of the human personality are revealed in all their disconcerting complexity'
– Anita Brookner

'A writer who, more than any other crime novelist, combined a high literary reputation with popular appeal'
– P. D. James

'A supreme writer . . . Unforgettable vividness'
– *Independent*

'Compelling, remorseless, brilliant'
– John Gray

'Extraordinary masterpieces of the twentieth century'
– John Banville

GEORGES SIMENON

The Shadow Puppet

Translated by ROS SCHWARTZ

PENGUIN BOOKS

PENGUIN CLASSICS

Published by the Penguin Group
Penguin Books Ltd, 80 Strand, London WC2R ORL, England
Penguin Group (USA) Inc., 375 Hudson Street, New York, New York 10014, USA
Penguin Group (Canada), 90 Eglinton Avenue East, Suite 700, Toronto, Ontario, Canada M4P 2Y3
 (a division of Pearson Penguin Canada Inc.)
Penguin Ireland, 25 St Stephen's Green, Dublin 2, Ireland (a division of Penguin Books Ltd)
Penguin Group (Australia), 707 Collins Street, Melbourne, Victoria 3008, Australia
 (a division of Pearson Australia Group Pty Ltd)
Penguin Books India Pvt Ltd, 11 Community Centre, Panchsheel Park, New Delhi – 110 017, India
Penguin Group (NZ), 67 Apollo Drive, Rosedale, Auckland 0632, New Zealand
 (a division of Pearson New Zealand Ltd)
Penguin Books (South Africa) (Pty) Ltd, Block D, Rosebank Office Park, 181 Jan Smuts Avenue,
Parktown North, Gauteng 2193, South Africa

Penguin Books Ltd, Registered Offices: 80 Strand, London WC2R ORL, England

www.penguin.com

First published in French as *L'ombre chinoise* by Fayard 1932
This translation first published 2014
001

Set in 12.5/15pt Dante
Typeset by Palimpsest Book Production Ltd, Falkirk, Stirlingshire
Printed in Great Britain by Clays Ltd, St Ives plc

ISBN: 978-0-141-39418-3

www.greenpenguin.co.uk

Contents

1. The Shadow Puppet

It was ten p.m. The iron gates of the public garden were locked and Place des Vosges was empty. Glistening tyre tracks on the asphalt, the continuous play of the fountains, leafless trees and the regular shapes of identical rooftops silhouetted against the sky.

There were few lights under the splendid arcades encircling the square. Only three or four shops. Inspector Maigret could see a family eating inside one of them, cluttered with beaded funeral wreaths.

He was trying to read the numbers above the doors, but he had barely passed the wreath shop when a diminutive form stepped out of the shadows.

'Is it you I just telephoned?'

She must have been watching out for a long time. Despite the November cold, she had not slipped on a coat over her apron. Her nose was red, her eyes anxious.

Less than 400 metres away, on the corner of Rue de Béarn, a uniformed police officer stood guard.

'Didn't you inform him?' grumbled Maigret.

'No! Because of Madame de Saint-Marc, who's about to give birth . . . Oh look! There's the doctor's car, he was asked to come straight away.'

There were three cars drawn up alongside the pavement, headlamps on, red rear lights. The sky, with its drifting clouds against a moonlit backdrop, had an ambiguous paleness. It felt as if the first snows were in the air.

The concierge turned under the archway at the building's entrance, from which hung a twenty-five-candlepower bulb covered in a film of dust.

'Let me explain. This is the courtyard – you have to cross it to get to all parts of the building, except for the two shops. This is my lodge on the left. Take no notice, I didn't have time to put the children to bed.'

There were two of them, a boy and a girl, in the untidy kitchen. But the concierge didn't go inside. She pointed to a long building, at the far end of the vast and beautifully proportioned courtyard.

'It's there. You'll see.'

Maigret was intrigued by this curious little woman, whose restless hands betrayed her febrility.

'There's someone on the phone asking for a detective chief inspector!' he had been told earlier at Quai des Orfèvres.

The voice on the other end was muffled. Several times he had repeated, 'Please speak up, I can't hear you.'

'I can't. I'm calling you from the tobacconist's. So—'
And a garbled message followed.

'You must come to 61, Place des Vosges right away . . . Yes . . . I think it's a murder, but don't tell anyone yet!'

And now the concierge was pointing at the tall first-floor windows. Behind the curtains, shadows could be seen coming and going.

'It's up there.'

'The murder?'

'No! Madame de Saint-Marc who's giving birth . . . Her first . . . She's not very strong. You understand?'

And the courtyard was even darker than Place des Vosges. It was illuminated by a single lamp on the wall. A staircase could just be made out on the other side of a glazed door, and there was the occasional lighted window.

'What about the murder?'

'I'm coming to that! Couchet's workers left at six o'clock—'

'Wait a moment. What is Couchet?'

'The building at the far end. A laboratory where they make serums. You must have heard of Doctor Rivière's Serums.'

'And that lighted window?'

'Wait. Today's the 30th, so Monsieur Couchet was there. He's in the habit of staying behind on his own after the offices have closed. I saw him through the window, sitting in his armchair. Look—'

A window with frosted-glass panes. A strange shadow, like that of a man slumped forward on his desk.

'Is that him?'

'Yes. Around eight o'clock, when I was emptying my rubbish bin, I glanced over in that direction. He was writing. You could clearly see the penholder or pencil in his hand.'

'What time did the murder—'

'Just a minute! I went upstairs to see how Madame de Saint-Marc was doing. I glanced over again when I came back down, and there he was, as he is now. Actually I thought he'd dozed off.'

Maigret was beginning to lose patience.

'Then, fifteen minutes later—'

'Yes! He was still in the same position! Get to the point.'

'That's all. I decided to check. I knocked on the office door. There was no answer so I went in. He's dead. There's blood everywhere.'

'Why didn't you go to the police? The police station is round the corner, in Rue de Béarn.'

'And they'd all have arrived in uniform! They'd have turned the place upside down! I told you that Madame de Saint-Marc—'

Maigret had both hands in his pockets, his pipe between his teeth. He looked up at the first-floor windows and had the impression that the birth was imminent, as there was even more to-ing and fro-ing. He heard a door opening, and footsteps on the stairs. A tall, broad shape appeared in the courtyard and the concierge, touching the inspector's arm, murmured reverentially, 'Monsieur de Saint-Marc. He's a former ambassador.'

The man, whose face was in shadow, paused, started walking again and stopped once more, constantly glancing up in the direction of his own windows.

'He must have been sent outside to wait. Already, earlier on . . . Come . . . Oh no! There they go again with their gramophone! And right above the Saint-Marcs, too!'

A smaller window, on the second floor, not so brightly lit. It was closed, and you could imagine, rather than hear, the music from a gramophone.

The concierge, all obsequious, jittery, red-eyed, her

fingers twitching, walked to the far end of the courtyard, pointed to a short flight of steps, a half-open door.

'You'll see him, on your left. I'd rather not go in there
again.'

An ordinary office. Light-coloured furniture. Plain wallpaper.

And a man in his mid-forties, sitting in an armchair, his
head on the scattered papers in front of him. He'd been
shot in the chest.

Maigret listened attentively: the concierge was still outside, waiting for him, and Monsieur de Saint-Marc was still
pacing up and down the courtyard. From time to time, an
omnibus rumbled past and the racket made the ensuing
silence seem all the more absolute.

The inspector touched nothing. He simply made sure
that the gun had not been left lying around the office,
stood surveying the scene for three or four minutes, puffing on his pipe, then he left, with a determined air.

'Well?'

The concierge was still there. She spoke in hushed tones.

'Nothing! He's dead!'

'Monsieur de Saint-Marc has just been called upstairs.'

There was a commotion in the apartment. Doors were
slamming. There was the sound of running footsteps.

'She's so frail!'

'Yes!' muttered Maigret, scratching the back of his neck.
'Only that's not the issue. Do you have any idea who could
have entered the office?'

'Me? How would I . . . ?'

'Excuse me, but from your lodge at the entrance to the building, you must see the residents coming and going.'

'I ought to! Now if the landlord gave me a decent lodge and put in proper lighting . . . I can only just hear footsteps and, yes, at night I see shadows . . . There are some footsteps I'm able to recognize.'

'Have you noticed anything unusual since six o'clock?'

'Nothing! Nearly all the residents came down to empty their rubbish. The bins are here, to the left of my lodge. Do you see the four dustbins? They're not allowed to come down before seven p.m.'

'And nobody came in via the archway?'

'How would I know? It's obvious you don't know this building. There are twenty-eight residents. Not counting the Couchet laboratory, where people are coming and going all the time.'

Footsteps in the entrance. A man in a bowler hat entered the courtyard, turned left and, going over to the dustbins, grabbed an empty bin. Despite the darkness, he must have spotted Maigret and the concierge, since he froze for a second, and then said, 'Nothing for me?'

'Nothing, Monsieur Martin.'

And Maigret asked, 'Who's that?'

'Monsieur Martin, a Registry Office official who lives on the second floor with his wife.'

'How come his rubbish bin—?'

'Nearly all of them do that when they have to go out. They bring the bin down on the way out and pick it up when they come back. Did you hear that?'

'What?'

'It sounded like . . . like a baby crying. If only those two up there would turn off that wretched gramophone! They know perfectly well that Madame de Saint-Marc's giving birth.'

She hurried over to the staircase, which someone was descending.

'Well, doctor? Is it a boy?'

'A girl.'

And the doctor left. He could be heard starting up his car and driving off.

Day-to-day life went on. The dark courtyard. The archway and its feeble bulb. The lighted windows and the vague sound of music from a gramophone.

The dead man was still in his office, all alone, his head resting on scattered papers.

Suddenly there was a scream from the second floor. A piercing shriek, like a desperate call for help. But the concierge didn't react. She sighed as she pushed open the door to her lodge, 'There goes the madwoman again.'

Then it was her turn to shout, because one of her kids had broken a plate. The light revealed the concierge's thin, tired face, her ageless body.

'When will all the formalities begin?' she asked.

The tobacconist's opposite was still open, and a few minutes later Maigret shut himself inside the telephone booth. He issued instructions in hushed tones.

'Yes, the public prosecutor . . . 61 . . . Almost on the corner of Rue de Turenne . . . and inform the forensics department . . . Hello! . . . Yes, I'm remaining at the scene.'

He walked a few steps and mechanically passed under the archway and ended up standing glumly in the middle of the courtyard, hunching his shoulders against the cold.

One by one the lighted windows went dark. The silhouette of the dead man could still be seen through the frosted glass like a Chinese shadow puppet.

A taxi pulled up. It wasn't the public prosecutor yet. A young woman crossed the courtyard with hurried steps, leaving a whiff of perfume in her wake, and pushed open the door to Couchet's office.

2. A Good Man

There was a whole succession of unfortunate moves that resulted in a comical situation. On discovering the body, the young woman wheeled round and caught sight of Maigret's tall form in the doorway. Automatically she associated two images: a dead man and a murderer.

Wide-eyed, her body tensed, she opened her mouth to scream for help, dropping her handbag.

Maigret had no time to argue. He seized her arm and put his hand over her mouth.

'Ssssh! You're mistaken! Police.'

Before his words sank in, she struggled and, being highly strung, tried to bite, kicking back with her heels.

There was a sound of silk ripping: her dress strap.

Finally, Maigret managed to reassure her. 'Hush,' he repeated, 'I'm from the police. We don't want to disturb the entire building.'

Silence, unusual in such situations, was the characteristic of this murder, as was the calmness, the twenty-eight residents all going about their ordinary business oblivious of the body.

The young woman adjusted her clothing and her hair.

'Were you his mistress?'

She shot Maigret a furious look as she rummaged for a pin to fix her strap.

'Had you arranged to meet him this evening?'

'At eight o'clock, at the Select. We were supposed to be having dinner together and then going to the theatre.'

'When he didn't turn up at eight, didn't you telephone him?'

'Yes! But the phone was off the hook.'

They both saw it at the same time, on the desk. The man must have knocked it over when he fell forward.

Footsteps in the courtyard, where that evening the slightest sounds were amplified, as if under a bell. The concierge called out from the threshold, to avoid seeing the body.

'Detective Chief Inspector . . . The local police—'

She did not like them. They arrived in groups of four or five, making no attempt to be discreet. One of them was telling a funny story. Another asked, on reaching the office, 'Where's the body?'

Since the local police chief was away, his deputy was standing in for him, so Maigret felt even more comfortable taking charge of operations.

'Leave your men outside. I'm waiting for the public prosecutor. It is preferable for the residents not to have any idea—'

And, while the deputy inspected the office, he turned once more to the young woman.

'What is your name?'

'Nine, Nine Moinard, but everyone calls me by my first name.'

'How long have you known Couchet?'

'Six months maybe.'

There was no need to ask her many questions. It was enough to watch her. A fairly pretty girl, still at the beginning of her career. Her outfit was from a quality fashion house, but her make-up, the way she held her bag and gloves and the aggressive look in her eyes gave away her music-hall background.

'Dancer?'

'I was at the Moulin Bleu.'

'What about now?'

'I'm with him.'

She hadn't had time to cry. Everything had happened too fast and the facts hadn't properly sunk in yet.

'Did he live with you?'

'Not exactly, because he was married. But—'

'Your address?'

'Hôtel Pigalle, Rue Pigalle.'

The police station deputy commented, 'In any case, no one can claim it was a burglary!'

'Why not?'

'Look! The safe's behind him! It's not locked, but the body is blocking the door!'

Nine, who had taken a small handkerchief out of her bag, sniffed and dabbed at her nostrils.

A moment later, the atmosphere changed. Cars screeching to a stop outside. Footsteps and voices in the courtyard. Then handshakes, questions, noisy discussions. The public prosecutor and his investigating team had arrived. The pathologist examined the body and the photographers set up their equipment.

For Maigret, it was an unpleasant wait. After exchanging

the obligatory pleasantries, he went outside, his hands in his pockets, lit his pipe and bumped into someone in the dark. It was the concierge, who could not stand by and let strangers run around her building without finding out what they were up to.

'What's your name?' Maigret asked her kindly.

'Madame Bourcier. Are these gentlemen going to be here long? Look! The light's gone out in Madame de Saint-Marc's bedroom, she must have gone to sleep, poor thing.'

Looking up at the building, the chief inspector noticed another light, a cream-coloured curtain and, behind it, a woman's silhouette. She was small and thin, like the concierge. You couldn't hear her voice, but even so, you could tell she was angry. Sometimes she would remain stock still, staring at an unseen person, then abruptly she would start speaking, gesticulating, taking a few steps forward.

'Who is that?'

'Madame Martin. You saw her husband return earlier, you know, the man who picked up his rubbish bin, the Registry Office official.'

'Are they in the habit of arguing?'

'They don't argue. She's the one who shouts. He doesn't dare open his mouth.'

From time to time, Maigret took a look inside the office where ten or so people were busy at work. Standing in the doorway, the prosecutor called the concierge.

'Who is Monsieur Couchet's second-in-command?'

'The manager, Monsieur Philippe. He doesn't live far away, he's on the Ile Saint-Louis.'

'Does he have a telephone?'

'He's bound to.'

There was a sound of voices speaking on the phone. Upstairs, Madame Martin's silhouette could no longer be seen against the curtain. However, a nondescript individual came down the stairs, furtively crossed the courtyard and went out into the street. Maigret recognized Monsieur Martin's bowler hat and putty-coloured overcoat.

It was midnight. The girls playing the gramophone switched off their lights. Apart from the office, the only light left on was on the first floor, in the Saint-Marcs' sitting room, where the former ambassador and the midwife were conversing in low voices, a faint odour of disinfectant in the air.

Despite the late hour, when Monsieur Philippe arrived, he was impeccably turned out, his dark, well-kempt beard, his hands gloved in grey suede. He was in his forties, the epitome of the serious-minded, well-brought-up intellectual.

He was certainly astonished, devastated even, by the news. But he seemed somehow to be holding back in his reaction.

'With the life he led,' he sighed.

'What life?'

'I refuse to speak ill of Monsieur Couchet. Besides, there's no ill to speak of. He was master of his own time—'

'Just a minute! Did Monsieur Couchet manage his company himself?'

'Neither hands-on nor hands-off. It was he who started

it up. But once it was up and running, he left me to handle everything. To the extent that sometimes I didn't see him for a fortnight. Take today, I waited for him till five o'clock. It's payday tomorrow. Monsieur Couchet was supposed to bring me the money to pay the staff's wages. Around 300,000 francs. At five o'clock, I had to go and I left a report for him on the desk.'

The typed report was still there, beneath the dead man's hand. A mundane report: a suggested rise for one worker and the sacking of one of the delivery men; a draft advert for the Latin American companies and so on.

'So the 300,000 francs should be here?' inquired Maigret.

'In the safe. The fact that Monsieur Couchet opened it proves it. He and I are the only two people who have the key and the code.'

But to open the safe, the body had to be moved, which could not be done until the photographers had finished their job. The pathologist was making his verbal report. Couchet had been hit by a bullet in the chest, which had severed the aorta, and death had been instantaneous. The distance between the killer and his victim was estimated at three metres. And lastly, the bullet was of the most common calibre: 6.35mm.

Monsieur Philippe explained some things to the examining magistrate.

'Here in Place des Vosges, we only have our laboratory, which is behind this office.'

He opened a door. They glimpsed a vast room with a glazed roof where thousands of test tubes stood in rows. Behind another door, Maigret thought he heard a noise.

'What's in there?'

'The guinea pigs. And to the right are the offices of the typists and the clerical staff. We have other premises in Pantin, from which most of the dispatching is done, for you probably know that Doctor Rivière's Serums are renowned worldwide.'

'Was it Couchet who launched them?'

'Yes! Doctor Rivière had no money. Couchet financed his research. Ten years ago he opened a laboratory which wasn't as big as this one yet.'

'Is Doctor Rivière still involved?'

'He died five years ago, in a road accident.'

At last Couchet's body was removed. But, the moment the safe was opened, there was consternation: all the money it had contained had vanished. Only business documents remained. Monsieur Philippe explained, 'Not only the 300,000 francs that Monsieur Couchet would definitely have brought, but another 60,000 francs held by a rubber band that had been cashed that afternoon and which I myself put in the safe!'

In the dead man's wallet, nothing. Or rather two numbered tickets for a theatre near Madeleine, the sight of which made Nine cry.

'They were for us! We were supposed to be going to the theatre.'

The forensics team was done. There was mounting chaos as the photographers folded up their unwieldy tripods, the pathologist washed his hands at a basin he'd come across in a closet, and the prosecutor's clerk yawned.

Despite all the goings-on around him, for a few moments Maigret had a sort of tête-à-tête with the dead man.

A vigorous man, on the short side, tubby. Like Nine, he had doubtless never entirely shed a certain vulgarity, despite his well-cut clothes, manicured nails and bespoke silk underwear.

His fair hair was thinning. His eyes were probably blue and had a slightly childlike expression.

'A good man!' sighed a voice behind him.

It was Nine, who was crying piteously and who took Maigret as witness, not daring to address the public prosecutor's more formal men.

'I swear to you he was a good man! Whenever he thought something would make me happy – and not just me, anybody – I've never seen a man give such generous tips. I even used to scold him, I told him people took him for a ride. And he'd reply, "So what?"'

Maigret asked gravely, 'Was he a cheerful man?'

'He seemed cheerful, but not deep down, if you know what I mean. It's hard to explain. He needed to be moving, doing something. If he sat still, he'd become broody or anxious.'

'What about his wife?'

'I only saw her once, from a distance. I don't have anything bad to say about her.'

'Where did Couchet live?'

'Boulevard Haussmann. But most of the time he'd go to Meulan, where he has a villa.'

Maigret abruptly turned his head, saw the concierge,

who did not dare come in. She was signalling to him, looking more unhappy than ever.

'Listen! He's coming down.'

'Who?'

'Monsieur de Saint-Marc. He must have heard all the commotion. Here he is. Just think! On a day like today!'

The former ambassador, in his dressing gown, was loath to approach. He had realized this was an investigation by the public prosecutor's office. Besides, the body on the stretcher passed close to him.

'What's going on?' he asked Maigret.

'A man's been murdered. Couchet, the owner of the serums laboratory.'

The chief inspector sensed that Monsieur de Saint-Marc had suddenly been struck by a thought, as if recalling something.

'Did you know him?'

'No. I mean, I knew of him.'

'And?'

'Nothing! I know nothing. What time did—'

'The murder must have been committed between eight and nine p.m.'

Monsieur de Saint-Marc sighed, smoothed his silver hair, nodded to Maigret and headed for the staircase leading up to his apartment.

The concierge had kept her distance. Then she went over to someone who was pacing back and forth under the archway, bent forward. When she came back to Maigret, he asked her, 'Who is that?'

'Monsieur Martin. He's looking for a glove he dropped.

He never goes out without his gloves, even to go and buy cigarettes fifty metres from here.'

Now searching around the dustbins, Monsieur Martin lit a few matches but eventually gave up and resigned himself to going back up to his apartment.

People were shaking hands in the courtyard. The public prosecutor left. The examining magistrate spoke briefly with Maigret.

'I'll leave you to get on with your job. Naturally you'll keep me posted.'

Monsieur Philippe, still looking as though he'd stepped out of the pages of a fashion magazine, bowed to the detective chief inspector.

'You no longer need me?'

'I'll see you tomorrow. You'll be at your office, I suppose?'

'At nine on the dot, as usual.'

Suddenly there was a moving scene, even though nothing particular happened. The courtyard was still plunged in shadow. A single lamp. And then the archway with its dusty light bulb.

Outside, cars revved up and glided over the asphalt, briefly picking out the trees of the Place des Vosges with their headlamps.

The body was no longer there. The office looked as if it had been ransacked. Nobody had thought to switch off the lights, and the laboratory was lit up as if in anticipation of a hard night's work.

And now there were three of them left in the middle of the courtyard, three very different people who an hour earlier had not known each other and who now seemed to be drawn to each other by an inexplicable kinship.

Or rather, they were like the family members who remain behind after a funeral when the rest of the guests have left.

At least this was Maigret's fleeting impression as he looked from Nine's exhausted face to the concierge's drawn features.

'Have you put your children to bed?'

'Yes, but they're not asleep. They're anxious, it's as if they can sense what's going on.'

Madame Bourcier had a question she wanted to ask, a question she was almost ashamed of, but which, for her, was capital.

'Do you think . . .'

Her gaze swept the courtyard and seemed to pause at each of the dark windows.

'. . . that . . . it's one of the residents?'

And now she was staring at the entrance, at the vast archway with its door constantly open, except after eleven p.m., which led from the courtyard to the street and gave the entire unknown world outside access to the building.

Nine meanwhile was looking uncomfortable, shooting the inspector covert glances.

'The investigation will doubtless answer your question, Madame Bourcier. For the time being, one thing seems certain, and that is that the person who stole the 360,000 francs is not the murderer. At least that is probable, since Monsieur Couchet's body was blocking the safe. By the way, were the lights on in the laboratory this evening?'

'Wait! Yes, I think so. But it wasn't as brightly lit as now. Monsieur Couchet must have switched on a light or two on his way to the toilet, which is right at the back of the building.'

Maigret went back to Couchet's office and switched off all the lights, while the concierge remained in the doorway, even though the body was no longer there. In the courtyard, the inspector found Nine waiting for him. He heard a noise somewhere above his head, the sound of an object swishing against a window pane.

But all the windows were shut, all the lights out.

Someone had moved, someone was watching from the shadows of a room.

'See you tomorrow, Madame Bourcier. I'll be here before the office opens.'

'I'll follow you. I have to lock the main door.'

Nine, standing on the edge of the pavement, remarked, 'I thought you had a car.'

She seemed reluctant to leave him. Looking at her feet, she added, 'Whereabouts do you live?'

'Very close by, Boulevard Richard-Lenoir.'

'The last Métro's gone, hasn't it?'

'I think so.'

'I'd like to tell you something.'

'Go ahead.'

She still did not dare meet his eye. Behind them, they could hear the concierge bolting the door and then her footsteps echoing as she went back to her lodge. There was not a soul in the square. The fountains were babbling. The town hall clock struck one.

'You're going to think that I'm imposing on . . . I don't know what you'll think. I told you that Raymond was very generous. He wasn't aware of the value of money. He used to give me anything I wanted. Do you understand?'

'And?'

'It's stupid, I asked for as little as possible. I'd wait until he thought of it. In any case, since he was with me nearly all the time, I didn't need anything. Tonight I was supposed to be having dinner with him. Well—'

'Broke?'

'It's not even that!' she protested. 'It's even more stupid! I was thinking of asking him for some money this evening. At lunchtime I paid a bill.'

This was excruciating for her. She kept an eye on Maigret, ready to clam up at the slightest hint of amusement.

'It never occurred to me that he wouldn't show up. I had a little money left in my bag. While I was waiting for him, at the Select, I ate oysters, and then lobster. I telephoned. It was only when I got here that I realized I only had enough to pay my taxi fare.'

'And at home?'

'I live in a hotel.'

'I'm asking if you have any money saved up.'

'Me?'

A nervous little laugh.

'What for? How could I have known? Even if I had, I wouldn't have wanted—'

Maigret sighed.

'Walk with me to Boulevard Beaumarchais. That's the

only place you'll find a taxi at this hour. What are you going to do?'

'Nothing. I—'

She shivered. True, she was dressed only in silk.

'Had he not made a will?'

'How would I know? Do you think people worry about such things when everything's fine? Raymond was a good man. I—'

She wept silently as she walked. The inspector slipped a 100-franc note into her hand, flagged down a passing car and, thrusting his fists in his pockets, muttered, 'See you tomorrow. You did say Hôtel Pigalle didn't you?'

When he got into bed, Madame Maigret woke up only long enough to murmur, sleepily, 'Did you at least have dinner?'

3. The Couple at Hôtel Pigalle

Leaving home at around eight a.m., Maigret had to choose between three pressing tasks: revisiting the premises at Place des Vosges and questioning the staff, paying a visit to Madame Couchet, who had been apprised of events by the local police, and lastly questioning Nine again.

On waking, he had telephoned police headquarters and given them the list of residents at number 61, as well as all the people connected either closely or remotely with the tragedy, so that when he went to his office, detailed information would be waiting for him.

The market on Boulevard Richard-Lenoir was in full swing. The weather was so cold that the inspector turned up the velvet collar of his overcoat. Place des Vosges was close by, but he had to walk there.

A tram going to Place Pigalle rumbled past and that prompted Maigret to make up his mind. He would see Nine first.

Of course, she was not up yet. The hotel receptionist recognized Maigret and expressed concern.

'She's not mixed up in any trouble, I hope? Such a quiet girl!'

'Does she have many visitors?'

'Only her friend.'

'The old one or the young one?'

'She only has one. He's neither young nor old.'

It was a comfortable hotel with a telephone in each room and a lift. Maigret was deposited on the third floor. He rapped on the door of room 27, heard someone thrashing around in bed, and then a voice stammer, 'What is it?'

'Open the door, Nine!'

A hand must have emerged from under the blankets and unbolted the door. Maigret entered the damp gloom, glimpsed the young woman's tired face, and went to draw the curtains.

'What time is it?'

'Not yet nine. Don't get up.'

She half-closed her eyes, because of the harsh light. In that state, she wasn't pretty and looked more like a country girl than a coquette. She ran her hand over her face a couple of times, eventually sat up in bed and placed a pillow behind her. Finally she picked up the telephone.

'Bring my breakfast!'

And, to Maigret, 'What a business! You're not too mad at me for scrounging off you last night? It's stupid! I'll have to sell my jewellery.'

'Have you got a lot?'

She gestured towards the dressing table, where a few rings, a bracelet and a watch lay in a promotional ashtray. Their combined value was around five thousand francs.

There was a knock at the door of the next room and Nine pricked up her ears, gave a vague smile as the knocking began again, more insistent this time.

'Who is that?' asked Maigret.

'My neighbours? I don't know! But if anyone manages to wake them up at this hour—'

'What do you mean?'

'Nothing! They're never up before four o'clock in the afternoon. That's when they wake up!'

'Do they take drugs?'

Her eyelashes fluttered a yes, but she hastened to add, 'You're not going to use what I tell you, are you?'

The door eventually opened. As did Nine's, and a chamber-maid brought in the tray with the coffee and croissants.

'May I?'

There were dark circles under her eyes and her night-dress revealed scrawny shoulders and small, not very firm breasts like those of a stunted child. As she dunked pieces of croissant in her *café au lait*, she continued to listen out, as if despite everything she did take an interest in what was going on next door.

'Will I be mixed up in all this?' she asked nevertheless. 'It would be awkward if they wrote about me in the news-papers! Especially for Madame Couchet.'

And, as someone was knocking on her door with urgent little taps, she shouted, 'Come in!'

A woman in her early thirties, who had slipped a fur coat over her nightdress and was barefoot, entered. She almost retreated on catching sight of Maigret's broad back, then she plucked up her courage and stammered, 'I didn't know you had company!'

Maigret shuddered at the sound of the languid voice that seemed to be struggling out of a furred mouth. He looked at the woman who was closing the door behind her and saw a face drained of colour, with puffy eyelids. A glance at Nine confirmed his guess. She was the drug addict from next door.

'What's happened?'

'Nothing! Roger has a visitor, so I took the liberty—'

She sat down on the end of the bed, dazed, and sighed as Nine had done, 'What time is it?'

'Nine o'clock!' said Maigret. 'Hmm, someone's been at the cocaine!'

'It's not cocaine, it's ether. Roger says it's better and that—'

She was cold. She got up to go and huddle by the radiator, gazing out of the window.

'It's going to rain again.'

The whole scene was gloomy, depressing. The comb on the dressing table was full of broken hairs. Nine's stockings lay on the floor.

'I'm in the way, aren't I? But apparently it's important. It's about Roger's father, who's just died.'

Maigret watched Nine and saw her suddenly knit her brow like someone who has just had an idea. At the same time, the woman who had just spoken raised her hand to her chin, thought for a moment and muttered, 'Oh my goodness!'

And the inspector asked, 'Do you know Roger's father?'

'I've never seen him. But . . . Hold on! Nine, nothing happened to your friend, did it?'

Nine and the inspector exchanged a glance.

'Why?'

'I don't know. It's all a bit muddled. I've just remembered

that Roger once told me that his father was a visitor here. It amused him, but he preferred not to bump into him and one time, when he heard someone coming up the stairs he rushed back into the room. I seem to recall that the person in question came in here.'

Nine stopped eating. The tray on her knees hindered her and her face betrayed her anxiety.

'His son?' she said slowly, staring at the dull glass rectangle of the window.

'Oh my goodness!' exclaimed the other woman. 'Then it's your friend who's dead! They say he was murdered.'

'Is Roger's surname Couchet?' asked Maigret.

'He's Roger Couchet, yes!'

Disconcerted, all three fell silent.

'What does he do?' continued the inspector after a long pause, during which a murmur of voices in the next room could be heard.

'Pardon?'

'What is his profession?'

The young woman snapped, 'You're from the police, aren't you?'

She was flustered. She might hold it against Nine for having lured her into a trap.

'The inspector's very kind!' said Nine, poking one leg out of the bed and leaning forward to pick up her stockings.

'I should have guessed! So then you already knew, before I came in.'

'I hadn't heard anything about Roger!' said Maigret. 'Now, I'll need you to give me some information about him.'

'I don't know anything. We've been together for barely three weeks.'

'What about before?'

'He was with a tall redhead who claimed to be a manicurist.'

'Does he work?'

The word 'work' created further discomfiture.

'I don't know.'

'In other words, he does nothing. Is he wealthy? Does he live extravagantly?'

'No! We nearly always have a six-franc set menu.'

'Does he often talk about his father?'

'I told you, he only mentioned him once.'

'Could you describe his visitor? Have you met him before?'

'No! He's a man . . . how can I say? To start with I thought he was a bailiff, that he'd come because Roger was in debt.'

'Is he well-dressed?'

'Hold on. I saw a bowler hat, a beige overcoat, gloves—'

Between the two rooms there was a communicating door concealed behind a curtain and probably locked. Maigret could have pressed his ear to it and overheard everything, but he was loath to do so in front of the two women.

Nine got dressed, contenting herself with wiping her face with a moistened towel by way of a wash. She was on edge. Her movements were jerky. It was clear that she was out of her depth and now she was expecting all sorts of trouble; she didn't have the strength to react or even to grasp the situation.

The other woman was calmer, perhaps because she was still under the influence of ether, perhaps because she had more experience of this sort of thing.

'What is your name?'

'Céline.'

'Do you have a profession?'

'I was a hairdresser doing home visits.'

'And on the vice squad's books?'

She shook her head, without showing annoyance. A murmur of voices could still be heard coming from next door.

Nine, who had slipped on a dress, gazed around the room and suddenly burst into tears, exclaiming, 'Oh God! Oh God!'

'It's a funny business!' said Céline slowly. 'And, if it really is a murder, they're going to keep pestering us.'

'Where were you last night at around eight p.m.?'

She cast her mind back.

'Hold on . . . Eight o'clock . . . Well, I was at the Cyrano.'

'Was Roger with you?'

'No. We can't be together all the time. I met him at midnight, at the tobacconist's in Rue Fontaine.'

'Did he tell you where he'd been?'

'I didn't ask.'

Through the window, Maigret could see Place Pigalle, its tiny garden, the nightclub signs. Suddenly, he straightened up and marched towards the door.

'Wait here for me, both of you!'

And he went out, knocked at the neighbouring door and turned the handle.

A man in pyjamas was sitting in the only armchair in the room, which reeked of ether despite the open window. Another man was pacing up and down, gesticulating. It was Monsieur Martin, whom Maigret had met twice the previous evening, in the courtyard at Place des Vosges.

'Ah, so you found your glove!'

Maigret was looking at the two hands of the official from the Registry Office, who turned so pale that the inspector thought for a moment that he was about to faint. His lips quivered. He attempted to speak but failed.

'I . . . I—'

The young man had not shaved. He had a pasty complexion, red-rimmed eyes and soft lips that were a sign of his spinelessness. He gulped water out of the tooth mug.

'Get a grip on yourself, Monsieur Martin! I hadn't expected to meet you here, especially at this hour when your office must have opened some time ago.'

Maigret studied him from head to toe. He had to make an effort not to take pity on him, such was the poor man's visible confusion.

From his shoes to his tie and his detachable white collar, Monsieur Martin was like a caricature of the archetypal civil servant. A dignified, neat and orderly official with a waxed moustache, not a speck of dust on his clothes, who no doubt deemed it shameful to go out without gloves.

Right now, he didn't know what to do with his hands, and his gaze searched the corners of the untidy room as if he hoped to find inspiration there.

'May I ask you a question, Monsieur Martin? How long have you known Roger Couchet?'

It was no longer fear, it was sheer terror.

'Me?'

'Yes, you!'

'Since . . . since my marriage!'

He said this as if it were self-evident.

'I don't understand!'

'Roger is my stepson, my wife's son.'

'And Raymond Couchet was his father?'

'Well yes . . . As—'

He grew more assured.

'My wife was Couchet's first wife. She has a son, Roger. After she got divorced, I married her.'

This had the effect of a gust of wind sweeping an overcast sky. The building in Place des Vosges was transformed by it. The nature of the events changed. Some points became clearer. Others, on the contrary, became muddier, more worrying.

To such an extent that Maigret no longer dared speak. He needed to muster his thoughts. He looked from one man to the other with mounting concern.

That very night, the concierge had asked him, looking up at all the windows that could be seen from the courtyard, *'Do you think it's one of the residents?'*

And her eyes finally came to rest on the archway. She hoped that the murderer had come in that way, that it was someone from outside.

Well it wasn't! The drama was indeed an internal affair! Maigret couldn't have said why, but he was convinced of it.

What drama? He hadn't the faintest idea!

Only he had a hunch that there were invisible threads linking points far apart in space, stretching from Place des Vosges to this hotel in Rue Pigalle, from the Martins' apartment to Couchet's laboratory, from Nine's room to that of the couple in an ether-induced stupor.

Perhaps the most disturbing thing was seeing Monsieur Martin tossed like a hapless spinning-top into this maze. He always wore gloves. His putty-coloured overcoat alone was an orderly, dignified statement. And his anxious look sought to alight somewhere without success.

'I came to tell Roger . . .' he stammered.

'Yes.'

Maigret looked him in the eyes, calmly, deeply, and almost expected to see Monsieur Martin shrink with fear.

'My wife told me that it would be best if we were the ones to . . .'

'I understand.'

'Roger is very—'

'Very sensitive.' Maigret took the words out of his mouth. 'An anxious boy.'

The young man, who was on his third glass of water, glared at him venomously. He must have been twenty-five, but his features were already careworn, his eyelids withered.

And yet he was still attractive, with a dark complexion and looks capable of seducing some women; everything about him was tinged with romanticism, even his weary, slightly nauseated air.

'Tell me, Roger Couchet, did you see your father often?'

'Sometimes.'

'Where?'

And Maigret's eyes bored into him.

'At his office, or at a restaurant.'

'When did you see him for the last time?'

'I don't know, a few weeks ago.'

'And did you ask him for money?'

'As always!'

'In other words, you were sponging off him?'

'He was wealthy enough to—'

'Just a moment! Where were you at around eight p.m. last night?'

There was no hesitation.

'At the Select,' he said with an ironic smile that meant, *Don't you think I can't see where this is leading!*

'What were you doing at the Select?'

'I was waiting for my father.'

'So, you needed money! And you knew that he'd be coming to the Select?'

'He was there nearly every evening with his mistress. And anyway, that afternoon I overheard her talking on the telephone. You can hear everything through these walls.'

'When you realized that your father wasn't coming, did it occur to you to go to his office in Place des Vosges?'

'No.'

Maigret picked up a photograph of the young man from the mantelpiece. It was surrounded by portraits of different women. He put it in his pocket, mumbling, 'May I?'

'If you wish.'

'You don't think—?' began Monsieur Martin.

'I don't think anything at all. Which reminds me I'd like to ask you some questions. How were relations between your household and Roger?'

'He didn't come often.'

'And when he did come?'

'He only stayed for a few minutes.'

'Is his mother aware of his lifestyle?'

'What do you mean?'

'Don't pretend to be stupid, Monsieur Martin. Does your wife know that her son lives in Montmartre and is a layabout?'

And the civil servant looked at the floor, embarrassed.

'I have often tried to persuade him to get a job,' he sighed.

This time, the young man started drumming impatiently on the table.

'You can see that I'm still in my pyjamas and that—'

'Would you tell me if you saw anyone you knew at the Select last night?'

'I saw Nine!'

'Did you say anything to her?'

'What? I have never spoken to her.'

'Where was she sitting?'

'The second table to the right of the bar.'

'Where did you find your glove, Monsieur Martin? If my memory serves me correctly, you were looking for it last night in the courtyard, near the dustbins.'

Monsieur Martin gave a strained little laugh.

'It was at home! Can you believe it, I had gone out with only one glove on and I hadn't noticed.'

'When you left Place des Vosges, where did you go?'

'I went for a walk along the embankment. I had a very bad headache.'

'Do you often go out for a walk at night without your wife?'

'Sometimes.'

This was agony for him. And he still didn't know what to do with his gloved hands.

'Are you going to your office now?'

'No! I telephoned to ask for the day off. I can't leave my wife in—'

'Well, go back to her, then!'

Maigret stayed put. The man was casting around for a dignified way of making his exit.

'Goodbye, Roger,' he gulped. 'I . . . I think you should go and see your mother.'

But Roger merely shrugged and gave Maigret an irritated look. Monsieur Martin's footsteps could be heard fading on the stairs.

The young man said nothing. His hand automatically picked up a bottle of ether from the bedside table and set it down further away.

'You have nothing to say?' the inspector asked slowly.

'Nothing!'

'Because, if you do want to make a statement, you'd better do so now rather than later.'

'I won't have anything to say to you later. No, actually I will! One thing I'll tell you right now, is that you're barking up the wrong tree.'

'By the way, since you didn't see your father last night, you must be short of money?'

'Too true!'

'Where are you going to find some?'

'Oh please don't worry about me. Do you mind?'

And he ran some water into the basin and started washing.

Maigret, to keep his countenance, took a few more steps and then left the room. He went next door, where the two women were waiting. Now it was Céline who was the most anxious. Nine was sitting in the wing chair slowly nibbling at a handkerchief and staring at the blank window with her big dreamy eyes.

'Well?' asked Roger's mistress.

'Nothing! You can go back to your room.'

'Is it really his father who—?'

And suddenly, she frowned.

'So does that mean he's going to inherit?'

Looking pensive, she left.

Outside on the pavement, Maigret asked Nine, 'Where are you going?'

A vague, dismissive wave, then, 'I'm going to the Moulin Bleu to see if they'll take me back.'

He watched her with avuncular interest.

'Were you fond of Couchet?'

'I told you yesterday, he was a good man. And there aren't many of those around, I can assure you! To think that some bastard—'

There were a couple of tears, then nothing.

'It's here,' she said pushing open a little door that was the stage entrance.

Maigret was thirsty and went into a bar for a beer. He had to go to Place des Vosges. The sight of a telephone reminded him that he hadn't yet dropped into Quai des Orfèvres and that there might be urgent post waiting on his desk.

He called the office boy.

'Is that you, Jean? Nothing for me? What? A lady who's been waiting for an hour? In mourning? It's not Madame Couchet? What? Madame Martin? I'm on my way.'

Madame Martin *in mourning*! And she'd been waiting for him at police headquarters for an hour!

All Maigret had seen of her so far was a shadow puppet, the comical, gesticulating shadow on the second-floor curtain the previous evening, whose mouth opened and shut, emitting a furious invective.

It happens all the time! the concierge had told him.

And the poor civil servant, who'd forgotten his glove and gone for a solitary walk along the dark banks of the Seine.

And when Maigret had left the courtyard, at one a.m., he'd heard a noise at a window.

He slowly climbed the dusty stairs, shook hands with a few colleagues in passing and put his head around the half-open door of the waiting room.

Ten green velvet armchairs. A table like a billiards table. On the wall, the roll of honour: 200 portraits of inspectors killed in the line of duty.

In the centre chair a lady in black sat very stiffly, one hand clutching her handbag with its silver clasp, the other resting on the handle of an umbrella.

Thin lips. A steady gaze staring straight ahead.

She did not move a muscle on sensing that she was being watched.

She sat and waited with a set expression.

4. The Second-Floor Window

She walked ahead of Maigret with that aggressive dignity of those for whom mockery is the worst calamity.

'Please sit down, madame!'

It was a clumsy, friendly Maigret, with a slightly vague look in his eyes who showed her into his office, indicating a chair bathed in light streaming in through the pale oblong window. She sat down, adopting exactly the same pose as in the waiting room.

A dignified pose, naturally! A fighting posture too. Her shoulders did not touch the back of the chair. And her black-gloved hand was poised to gesticulate without letting go of the handbag, which would swing through the air.

He, on the other hand, sat in an armchair. It was tilted back, and he sprawled in a rather crude position, puffing avidly on his pipe.

'I imagine, Detective Chief Inspector, that you are wondering why I—'

'No!'

It wasn't malice that made Maigret throw her off balance like that the minute they met. It wasn't a coincidence either. He knew it was necessary.

Madame Martin jumped, or rather her chest stiffened.

'What do you mean? I don't imagine you were expecting—'

'Oh yes, I was!'

And he smiled at her good-naturedly. Suddenly, her fingers were ill at ease in her black woollen gloves. Her sharp gaze swept the room and then something occurred to Madame Martin.

'Have you received an anonymous letter?'

It was a statement as much as a question, with a false air of certainty, which made the inspector smile all the more, because this again was a characteristic trait that fitted in with everything he already knew about the woman sitting in his office.

'I've not received any anonymous letter.'

She shook her head dubiously.

'You won't have me believe—'

She was straight out of a family photo album. Physically, she was a perfect match for the Registry Office official she had married.

It was easy to imagine them strolling up the Champs-Élysées on Sunday afternoons: Madame Martin's black, twitchy back, her hat always skew-whiff because of her bun, walking with the hurried pace of an active woman and that jerk of her chin to underline her emphatic words; Monsieur Martin's putty-coloured overcoat, his leather gloves and walking stick, and his peaceful, assured gait, his attempts at a leisurely promenade, stopping to gaze at the window displays.

'Did you have mourning clothes at home?' murmured Maigret snidely, exhaling a big cloud of smoke.

'My sister died three years ago . . . I mean my sister in Blois, the one who married a police inspector. You see that—'

'That—?'

Nothing. She was warning him. It was time to make him aware that she wasn't just anyone!

She was on edge, because the entire speech she had rehearsed was pointless, and it was the fault of this burly inspector.

'When did you hear about the death of your first husband?'

'Why . . . this morning, like everyone else! It was the concierge who told me you were handling this case and, seeing as my situation is rather awkward . . . You can't possibly understand.'

'I think I can! By the way, didn't your son visit you yesterday afternoon?'

'What are you insinuating?'

'Nothing. It's a simple question.'

'The concierge will tell you that he hasn't been to see me for at least three weeks.'

She spoke sharply. The look in her eyes more aggressive. Had Maigret perhaps been wrong not to let her make her speech?

'I'm delighted that you've come to see me, as it shows great delicacy and—'

The mere word 'delicacy' caused something in the woman's grey eyes to change, and she bowed her head by way of thanks.

'Some situations are very painful,' she said. 'Not everybody understands. Even my husband, who advised me not to wear mourning! Mind you, I'm wearing it without wearing it. No veil. No crape band. Just black clothes.'

He nodded his chin and put his pipe down on the table.

'Just because we're divorced and Raymond made me unhappy, it doesn't mean that I must—'

She was regaining her assurance and imperceptibly launching into her prepared speech.

'Especially in a large building like ours, where there are twenty-eight households. And what households! I'm not talking about the people on the first floor. And even then! Although Monsieur de Saint-Marc is well-bred, his wife's something else, she wouldn't say hello to her neighbours for all the gold in the world. When one has been properly brought up, it's distressing to—'

'Were you born in Paris?'

'My father was a confectioner in Meaux.'

'How old were you when you married Couchet?'

'I was twenty. Of course, my parents wouldn't let me serve in the shop. In those days, Couchet used to travel. He stated that he earned a very good living, that he could make a woman happy.'

Her gaze hardened as she sought reassurance that there was no threat of mockery from Maigret.

'I'd rather not tell you how much he made me suffer! All the money he earned he lost in ridiculous gambles. He claimed he was growing rich, we moved home three times a year, and by the time my son was born, we had no savings at all. It was my mother who had to pay for the layette.'

Finally she rested her umbrella against the desk. Maigret mused that she must have been speaking with the same sharp vehemence the previous evening when he'd seen her shadow against the curtain.

'When a man isn't capable of feeding a wife, he has no

business getting married! That's what I say. And especially when he has no pride left. I hardly dare tell you all the jobs Couchet's had. I told him to look for a proper position, with a pension attached, in the civil service, for example. At least if anything happened to him, I wouldn't be left destitute. But no! He even ended up following the Tour de France as some sort of dogsbody. His job was to organize food for the cyclists, or something of the sort. And he came back without a *sou*! That's the man he was. And that's the life I had.'

'Where did you live?'

'In Nanterre. Because we couldn't even afford to live in the city. Did you know Couchet? He wasn't worried, oh no! He wasn't ashamed! He wasn't anxious! He said he was born to make lots of money and that's what he would do. After bicycles, it was watch chains. No! You'll never guess! Watch chains which he sold from a stall at funfairs, monsieur! And my sisters no longer dared go to the Neuilly fair for fear of coming across him selling his watch chains.'

'Were you the one who asked for a divorce?'

She modestly bowed her head, but her features remained tense.

'Monsieur Martin lived in the same apartment block as us. He was younger then. He had a good job in the civil service. Couchet left me on my own all the time while he went off gallivanting. Oh! It was all very above-board! I gave my husband a piece of my mind. The divorce was requested by mutual consent for incompatibility of temperaments. All Couchet had to give me was maintenance for the boy. And Martin and I waited a year before getting married.'

Now she was fidgeting on her chair. Her fingers plucked at the silver clasp on her bag.

'You see, I've always been unlucky. At first, Couchet didn't even pay the maintenance money regularly. And, for a sensitive woman, it's painful to see her second husband paying for the upkeep of a child who's not his.'

No, Maigret was not asleep, even though his eyes were half-closed and his pipe had gone out.

This was becoming more and more harrowing. The woman's eyes started brimming. Her lips began to tremble in a disconcerting manner.

'No one else knows what I've suffered. I put Roger through school. I wanted to give him a good education. He wasn't like his father. He was affectionate, caring . . . When he was seventeen, Martin found him a job in a bank, so he could learn the profession. But that's when he met Couchet, I don't know where.'

'And he got into the habit of asking his father for money?'

'Couchet had always refused to give me anything, mind you! For me, everything was too expensive! I made my own dresses and I wore the same hat for three years.'

'And he gave Roger everything he asked for?'

'He corrupted him! Roger left home to go and live on his own. He still comes to see me from time to time. But he also used to go and see his father.'

'How long have you lived at Place des Vosges?'

'About eight years. When we found the apartment, we didn't even know that Couchet was in serums. Martin wanted to move out. That was all I needed! If it was up to anyone to move, it should have been Couchet, shouldn't it? Couchet grown rich somehow or other. I'd see him rolling up in a chauffeur-driven car! He had a chauffeur, you know. I saw his wife.'

'At her house?'

'I watched her from the street, to see what she looked like. I'd rather not say anything. She's nothing special, in any case, despite her airs and graces and her astrakhan coat.'

Maigret drew his hand across his forehead. This was becoming obsessive. He'd been staring at the same face for fifteen minutes and right now he felt that he would never be able to get it out of his mind.

A thin face, drained of colour, with fine features, which seemed set in an expression of resigned suffering.

And that too reminded him of certain family portraits, even of his own family. As a child, he had had an aunt, plumper than Madame Martin, but who also complained all the time. When she visited his family, he knew that the moment she sat down she'd pull a handkerchief out of her bag:

'My poor Hermance!' she'd begin. 'What a life! You'll never guess what Pierre's done now.'

And she had that same mobile mask, those too-thin lips and eyes that sometimes registered a flicker of disarray.

Madame Martin suddenly lost her train of thought. She grew flustered.

'Now, you must understand my situation. Naturally, Couchet remarried. All the same, I was his wife, I shared his early life, in other words, the hardest years. Whereas she's just a doll.'

'Are you saying you have a claim on his estate?'

'Me!' she cried indignantly, 'I wouldn't touch his money with a barge pole! We're not rich. Martin lacks drive, he doesn't know how to put himself forward and he allows the grass to grow under his feet while less clever colleagues . . . but even if I had to be a cleaner to make a living, I wouldn't want—'

'Did you send your husband to tell Roger?'

She didn't blanch, because it wasn't possible. Her complexion remained uniformly ashen. But her gaze clouded.

'How do you know?'

And suddenly, indignant, 'We're not being followed, I hope? Tell me! That would be outrageous! And, if it is the case, I shall have no hesitation in taking this to the highest authority.'

'Calm down, madame . . . I didn't say any such thing. I ran into Monsieur Martin by chance this morning.'

But she was still mistrustful, staring at the chief inspector with dislike.

'I'm going to end up wishing I hadn't come. One tries too hard to do the right thing! And, instead of being grateful—'

'I assure you I'm infinitely grateful to you for coming to see me.'

She still had the feeling that something was amiss. She felt terrified by this big man with broad shoulders and a hunched neck who was looking at her with innocent eyes as if his mind were completely vacant.

'Besides,' she said shrilly, 'it's better you hear it from me than from the concierge . . . You'd have found out one way or another—'

'. . . That you are the first Madame Couchet.'

'Have you seen Madame Couchet number two?'

Maigret struggled to repress a smile.

'Not yet.'

'Oh! She'll weep crocodile tears. Mind you, she'll be all right now, with the millions Couchet made.'

And suddenly she began to cry, her lower lip came up, transforming her face, softening its sharp angles.

'She didn't even know him when he was struggling, when he needed a wife to support and encourage him—'

From time to time, a muffled sob, barely audible, escaped from her slender throat encircled by a silk moiré ribbon.

She rose and glanced around to make sure she hadn't forgotten anything. She sniffed, 'But none of that counts.'

A bitter smile, beneath her tears.

'Well, anyhow, I've done my duty. I don't know what you think of me, but—'

'I assure you that—'

He would have been hard put to continue if she had not finished the sentence for him.

'I don't care. I've got a clear conscience! It's not everyone who can say as much.'

She was missing something but she didn't know what. She glanced round the room again and shook one hand as if surprised to find it empty.

Maigret had risen to his feet and saw her to the door.

'Thank you for coming to see me.'

'I did what I felt was my duty.'

She was in the corridor where inspectors were chatting and laughing. She swept past the group, head held high, without looking round.

And Maigret, his door closed, walked over to the window and flung it wide open, despite the cold. He felt weary, like after a tough criminal interrogation. In particular he felt that sort of vague unease one feels when forced to consider certain aspects of life one generally prefers to ignore.

It wasn't dramatic. It wasn't horrifying.

She hadn't said anything extraordinary. She hadn't given Maigret any new leads.

Even so, the conversation with her had left him with a faint feeling of disgust.

On a corner of the desk, the police gazette lay open, showing twenty or so photographs of wanted individuals. Most of them faces of thugs. Faces that bore the scars of degeneracy.

Ernst Strowitz, sentenced in absentia by the Caen tribunal for the murder of a farmer's wife on the Route de Bénouville . . .

And the warning, in red:

Dangerous. Still armed.

A fellow who would not sell himself cheaply. Well! Maigret would have preferred that to all this syrupy greyness, to these family sagas, to this still inexplicable murder, which he found mind-boggling.

His head was full of images: he pictured the Martins out

for their Sunday stroll. The putty-coloured overcoat and the black silk ribbon around the woman's neck.

He rang a bell. Jean appeared, and Maigret sent him to fetch the records of all those connected to the murder case that he had requested.

There wasn't much. Nine had been arrested once, only once, in Montmartre, in a raid, and had been released after proving that she did not make her living from prostitution.

As for the Couchet boy, he was being watched by the vice squad, which suspected him of drug trafficking. But they had never been able to pin anything on him.

A call to the vice squad. Céline, whose surname was Loiseau and who was born in Saint-Amand-Montrond, was well known to them. She had a record. They picked her up fairly frequently.

'She's not a bad girl!' said the brigadier. 'Most of the time she's content with one or two regular friends. It's only when she ends up back on the street that we find her.'

Jean had not left the room and was signalling to Maigret.

'That lady forgot her umbrella!'

'I know.'

'Oh!'

'Yes, I need it.'

And the inspector rose with a sigh, went over and shut the window, and stood with his back to the fire in his habitual thinking posture.

An hour later, he was able to make a mental summary of the notes he'd received from various departments and which were spread out on his desk.

First of all, the result of the autopsy confirming the pathologist's theory: the shot had been fired from around three metres away and death had been instantaneous. The dead man's stomach contained a small amount of alcohol, but no food.

The photographs from the Criminal Records Office, located under the eaves of the Palais de Justice, showed that no fingerprint matches had been found.

And lastly, the Crédit Lyonnais confirmed that at around three p.m., Couchet, who was a well-known customer, had dropped into the bank's head office and withdrawn 300,000 francs in new bills, as was customary on the penultimate day of each month.

It was pretty much established that on arriving at Place des Vosges, Couchet had placed the 300,000 in the safe, alongside the 60,000 already in there.

And since he still had work to do, he had not locked the safe again but was leaning against it.

The lights in the laboratory suggested that at some point he had left the office, either to inspect another part of the building or, more likely, to go to the toilet.

Had the money still been in the safe when he sat down at his desk again?

Probably not, for if it had been, the murderer would have had to move the body to open the heavy door and take the wads of cash.

So much for the technicalities. But was it a *thief and murderer* or a *murderer* and a *thief* operating separately?

Maigret spent ten minutes with the examining magistrate,

apprising him of the progress to date. Then, since it was just after noon, he set off home, hunching his shoulders, a sign he was in a bad mood.

'Is it you who's investigating the Place des Vosges case?' asked his wife, who had read the newspaper.

'It is!'

And Maigret had a very particular way of sitting down and looking at Madame Maigret, with a mixture of increased affection and a hint of anxiety.

He could still picture Madame Martin's thin face, black clothes and sorrowful eyes.

And those tears that had suddenly welled up, then disappeared, as if consumed by an inner fire, only to flow again a little later!

Madame Couchet who had furs . . . Madame Martin who didn't . . . Couchet who fed the Tour de France cyclists while his first wife had to wear the same hat for three years.

And what about the son . . . And the bottle of ether on the bedside table in Hôtel Pigalle?

And Céline, who only went on the streets periodically, when she didn't have a regular boyfriend?

And Nine?

'You don't look happy . . . You don't look well, you look as though you're coming down with a cold.'

It was true! Maigret could feel a tickle in his nostrils and his head was like cotton wool.

'What's that umbrella you've brought in? It's horrible!'

Madame Martin's umbrella! The Martins, putty-coloured

overcoat and black silk dress, out for a Sunday stroll down the Champs-Élysées!

'It's nothing. I don't know what time I'll be back.'

There are impressions that cannot be explained: something felt wrong, something that emanated from the façade itself.

Was it the flurry of activity in the shop that made beaded funeral wreaths? Of course, the residents must have clubbed together to buy a wreath.

Or the anxiety on the face of the ladies' hairdresser on the other side of the archway whose salon faced on to the street?

In any case, there was something unsavoury about the building that day. And, since it was four p.m. and beginning to grow dark, the feeble little lamp under the archway was already lit.

Opposite, the park keeper was locking the gates. In the Saint-Marcs' first-floor apartment, the manservant was drawing the curtains, slowly, meticulously.

When Maigret knocked at the door of the concierge's lodge, he found Madame Bourcier telling the whole story to a Dufayel credit collector in the store's navy blue livery who wore a little inkwell pendant on a chain around his neck.

'This is a respectable residence where nothing has ever happened . . . Sssh! . . . Here comes the inspector.'

She vaguely had something in common with Madame Martin, in that both women were ageless, and sexless. And both had suffered, or considered they had.

Except that the concierge seemed more resigned, displaying an almost animal acceptance of her fate.

'Jojo . . . Lili . . . Don't stand in the way . . . Good evening, Detective Chief Inspector . . . I was expecting you this morning . . . What a business! . . . I thought it was the right thing to do to go round to all the residents to ask them to club together for a wreath. Do we know when the funeral will be? . . . Oh, by the way . . . Madame de Saint-Marc . . . you know! . . . Please don't say anything to her . . . Monsieur de Saint-Marc came by this morning . . . He doesn't want her upset, in her condition.'

In the dusky light of the courtyard, the two lamps, the one hanging in the archway and the one on the wall, threw long yellow lines.

'Madame Martin's apartment?' asked Maigret.

'Second floor, third door on the right, after the bend.'

Maigret recognized the window, where a light was on, but there was no shadow against the curtain.

A clatter of typewriters could be heard coming from the offices. A delivery man arrived.

'Doctor Rivière's Serums?'

'At the back of the courtyard. Right-hand door. Jojo! Leave your sister alone!'

Maigret started walking up the stairs, Madame Martin's umbrella under his arm. The building had been renovated up to the first floor, the walls repainted and the stairs varnished.

From the second floor, it was a different world – grubby walls and a rough floor. The apartment doors were painted an ugly brown and had either name cards tacked on to them or little spun aluminium plates.

A calling card at three francs a hundred: *Monsieur and Madame Edgar Martin*. To the right, a three-colour braided bell-pull with a silk tassel. When Maigret yanked it, a reedy bell rang in the hollowness of the apartment. Then there were rapid footsteps. A voice asked, 'Who is it?'

'I've brought back your umbrella.'

The door opened. The entrance hall was reduced to one square metre with a coat stand from which the putty-coloured overcoat hung. Directly opposite, the open door of a room, part living room, part dining room, with a wireless set on a sideboard.

'Forgive me for the intrusion. This morning you left this umbrella in my office.'

'There you go! And I was convinced I'd left it on the bus. I was saying to Martin—'

Maigret did not smile. He was used to women who were in the habit of calling their husbands by their surnames.

Martin was there, in his striped trousers over which he'd slipped a chocolate-coloured, coarse-cloth smoking jacket.

'Do come in.'

'I wouldn't want to disturb you.'

'You never disturb people who have nothing to hide!'

The primordial characteristic of a home is probably its smell. Here, the smell was indistinct, a blend of caustic soda, cooking and musty old clothes.

A canary was hopping about in a cage, occasionally spraying a drop of water.

'Offer the detective chief inspector the armchair.'

The armchair! There was only one, a high-backed Voltaire leather armchair so dark that it looked black.

And Madame Martin, very different from how she had been that morning, simpered, 'You'll have a drink, won't you . . . Oh you must! Martin! Pour an aperitif.'

Martin was flustered. Perhaps there was nothing to drink? Perhaps they were nearly out?

'No thank you, madame. I never drink on an empty stomach.'

'But you have the time—'

It was sad. So sad that it almost made you want to give up on being a man, on living on this earth, even though the sun shines over it for several hours a day and there are real birds flying freely!

These people didn't seem very fond of light, for the three electric bulbs were carefully shrouded in heavy, coloured shades that let only the tiniest amount of light through.

'Caustic soda mainly,' thought Maigret.

That was the dominant *smell*! What's more, the surface of the solid oak table was polished as smooth as an ice rink.

Monsieur Martin wore the smile of a man entertaining.

'You must have a marvellous view over the Place des Vosges, which is the only square of its kind in Paris,' said Maigret, who was perfectly aware that the windows over-looked the courtyard.

'No! The apartments at the front, on the second floor, have very low ceilings, because of the architectural style . . . All the buildings around the square are classed as historical monuments, you know. We can't change anything, which is a great shame! We've been wanting to put in a bathroom for years and—'

Maigret had walked over to the window. He casually tweaked the shadow-puppet blind. And stood stock still, so stunned that he forgot to make polite conversation.

Facing him were the Couchet firm's offices and laboratory.

From downstairs he had noticed that there were frosted-glass windows, but from up here, he saw that only the lower panes were frosted. The others were clear, transparent, washed two or three times a week by the cleaning women.

There was a clear view of the spot where Couchet had been killed, and of Monsieur Philippe signing the typed letters that his secretary was handing to him one at a time. He could see the lock on the safe.

And the communicating door to the laboratory stood ajar. Through the laboratory windows, a row of women in white overalls, sitting at a massive bench, could be seen packing glass tubes.

Each woman had a particular task. The first took the bare tubes from a basket and the ninth passed the neat packages with their patient information leaflets to an office worker, in other words, goods ready to be delivered to the pharmacists.

'Pour him a drink anyway,' said Madame Martin's voice behind Maigret.

And her husband busied himself opening a cupboard with a clinking of glasses.

'Just a thimbleful of Vermouth, Detective Chief Inspector! . . . No doubt Madame Couchet is able to offer you cocktails—'

And Madame Martin gave a peeved smile, as if her lips were barbs.

5. The Madwoman

Glass in hand, watching Madame Martin closely, Maigret said, 'If only you'd been looking out of the window yesterday evening, my investigation would be over! Because from here it is impossible not to see everything that goes on in Couchet's office.'

His voice and manner contained no insinuations. He sipped his Vermouth and carried on chatting.

'I'd even say that this case would have been one of the most unusual instances of witnessing a criminal act. Someone who was present at a murder from a distance! What am I saying? With binoculars, you'd be able to see the lips of the speakers so clearly that you could work out what they were saying.'

Not knowing what to think, Madame Martin remained guarded, a vague smile frozen on her pale lips.

'But also, how upsetting for you! Standing at your window, minding your own business, and suddenly seeing someone threatening your ex-husband! Even worse, for the scenario must have been more complicated than that. I can picture Couchet all alone, absorbed in his accounts. He gets up and goes to the toilet. When he comes back, someone has ransacked the safe but hasn't managed to get away. But there is one odd detail, which is that Couchet sat down again. True, perhaps he knew the thief? . . . He speaks to him . . . He chides him, asks him to hand back the money—'

'The only thing is, I'd have had to be at the window,' said Madame Martin.

'Perhaps other windows on this floor afford the same view? Who lives on your right?'

'Two girls and their mother . . . The ones who play records every night.'

Just then came a scream, which Maigret had heard before. He said nothing at first, then murmured, 'That's the madwoman, isn't it?'

'Sssh!' said Madame Martin tiptoeing over to the door.

She flung it open and in the dimly lit corridor the shape of a woman beating a hasty retreat could be seen.

'Old cat!' grumbled Madame Martin loudly enough to be heard by the receding figure.

Coming back into the room, furious, she explained, 'It's old Mathilde! A former cook. Did you see her? She looks like a fat toad! She lives in the room next door with her sister, who's mad. I don't know which one's the ugliest. The mad one hasn't left her room once in all the years we've had this apartment.'

'Why does she scream like that?'

'Why indeed! She screams when she's left alone in the dark. She's afraid, like a child. She screams . . . I've finally worked out what's going on. From morning till night, old Mathilde roams the corridors. You're bound to come across her lurking behind a door. And when you catch her, she's not even embarrassed . . . She wanders off with her ugly, placid grin. You don't feel at home here any more, you have to talk in whispers if you want to discuss private matters. I just caught her at it, didn't I? Well, I bet she's already back.'

'It's not very pleasant,' agreed Maigret. 'But can't the landlord do anything about it?'

'He's done his best to throw them out, but unfortunately there are laws. To say nothing of the fact that it's both unhealthy and repugnant, those two old women in one tiny room! I bet they never wash.'

Maigret had grabbed his hat.

'Forgive me for having disturbed you. It's time for me to go.'

Now he had a clear picture of the apartment in his mind, from the doilies to the calendars on the walls.

'Be very quiet and you'll catch the old lady at it.'

That was not entirely the case. She wasn't in the corridor, but behind her half-open door, like a plump spider waiting to ambush her prey. She must have been disconcerted when the inspector greeted her politely as he walked past.

Aperitif time found Maigret sitting in the Select, not far from the American bar where all the talk was of horse-racing. When the waiter came over, he showed him the photo of Roger Couchet, which he had 'borrowed' from the young man that morning.

'Do you know this young man?'

The waiter looked surprised.

'That's strange.'

'What's strange?'

'He left not even fifteen minutes ago. He was sitting at this table! I wouldn't have noticed him except that instead of telling me what he wanted to drink, he said, "Same as yesterday"! But I didn't recall seeing him, so I said, "Can you remind me what that was?" "A gin-fizz, remember?", and that's the oddest part. Because I'm sure I didn't serve a single gin-fizz yesterday evening.

'He stayed for a few minutes and then he left . . . It's strange that you should come in just now and show me his photograph.'

It wasn't strange at all. Roger had been determined to establish that he had been at the Select the previous evening, as he had told Maigret. He had used quite a clever trick but his mistake had been to choose a drink that was out of the ordinary.

A few minutes later, Nine came in, looking downcast, and sat at the table closest to the bar. Then, spotting Maigret, she rose, dithered, and came over to him.

'Did you want to talk to me?' she asked.

'Not especially. Actually yes! I'd like to ask you a question. You come here almost every evening, don't you?'

'Raymond always asked me to meet him here.'

'Do you have a regular table?'

'Over there, where I sat when I came in.'

'Were you there yesterday?'

'Yes, why?'

'And do you remember seeing the original of this portrait?'

She looked at the photo of Roger and murmured, 'But that's my next-door neighbour!'

'Yes, he's Couchet's son.'

Troubled by this coincidence, her eyes opened wide as she wondered what it meant.

'He came over shortly after you left this morning. I'd just got back from the Moulin Bleu.'

'What did he want?'

'He asked me if I had an aspirin for Céline, who was ill.'

'And did they hire you at the theatre?'

'I have to go there this evening. One of the dancers is injured. If she's not better, I'll stand in for her and perhaps they'll give me a permanent job.'

She lowered her voice and went on, 'I have the hundred francs. Give me your hand.'

And that gesture revealed her entire character. She didn't want to give Maigret the money in public. She was afraid of embarrassing him! So she had the note folded into a tiny oblong in the palm of her hand. She passed it to him as if he were a gigolo.

'Thank you, you were so kind.'

She sounded despondent. She looked about her without taking the slightest interest in the pantomime of people coming and going. She gave a wan smile and said, 'The head waiter's looking at us. He's wondering why I'm with you. He must think I've already replaced Raymond . . . This must be awkward for you!'

'Would you like a drink?'

'No, thank you,' she said discreetly. 'If ever you need me . . . At the Moulin Bleu, my stage name is Élyane . . . Do you know where the stage door is, in Rue Fontaine?'

*

It wasn't too difficult. Maigret rang the bell of the apartment on Boulevard Haussmann a few minutes before dinner time. The moment he stepped inside there was an overpowering smell of chrysanthemums. The maid who opened the door walked on tiptoe.

She thought the inspector simply wanted to leave his card and wordlessly she showed him to the room where the body was laid out, draped in black. By the door were numerous calling cards on a Louis XVI tray.

The body was already in its casket, which was invisible under all the flowers.

In a corner, a tall, very distinguished young man in mourning nodded briefly at Maigret.

Opposite him kneeled a woman in her fifties, with coarse features, dressed like a countrywoman in her Sunday best.

The inspector went up to the young man.

'May I see Madame Couchet?'

'I'll ask my sister if she can see you. You are Monsieur—?'

'Maigret! The detective chief inspector in charge of the investigation.'

The countrywoman stayed where she was. A few moments later, the young man returned and steered his guest through the apartment.

Apart from the all-pervasive scent of flowers, the rooms retained their usual look. It was a magnificent late nineteenth-century apartment, like most of the buildings on Boulevard Haussmann. Vast rooms. Slightly over-ornate ceilings and doors.

And classy period furniture. In the drawing room, a

monumental crystal chandelier tinkled when people walked underneath it.

Madame Couchet sat flanked by three people, whom she introduced. First of all, the young man in mourning:

'My brother, Henry Dormoy, barrister.'

Then a gentleman of a certain age:

'Colonel Dormoy, my uncle.'

And lastly, a lady with magnificent silver hair:

'My mother.'

And all of them, in mourning, looked extremely distinguished. The table had not yet been cleared of the tea things and there was toast and cakes.

'Please sit down.'

'One question, if I may. The lady who is sitting with the body—'

'My husband's sister,' replied Madame Couchet. 'She arrived this morning from Saint-Amand.'

Maigret did not smile, but he understood. He clearly sensed that they were not overly keen to see the Couchet family turn up, dressed like bumpkins or got up like petty bourgeois.

There were the relatives on the husband's side and the relatives on the Dormoy side.

The Dormoys were elegant, discreet. For a start, everyone was wearing black.

From the Couchets, for the moment there was only this countrywoman, whose black silk blouse was straining under the arms.

'May I have a few words with you in private, madame?'

She apologized to her family, who made to leave the drawing room.

'Please stay, we'll go into the yellow boudoir.'

She had been crying, there was no doubt. Then she had powdered her face and her puffy eyelids barely showed. There was a note of genuine weariness in her voice.

'You haven't received any unexpected visits today, have you?'

She looked up, vexed.

'How do you know? Yes, early this afternoon, my stepson came.'

'Had you met him before?'

'Very briefly. He used to go and see my husband at his office. But we ran into him at the theatre on one occasion and Raymond introduced us.'

'What was the purpose of his visit?'

Embarrassed, she looked away.

'He wanted to know if we'd found a will. He also asked me the name of my lawyer so he could contact him concerning the formalities.'

She sighed by way of an apology for all this unpleasantness.

'He's entitled to. I think that half the inheritance goes to him, and I don't intend to stand in his way.'

'May I ask a few personal questions? When you married Couchet, was he already wealthy?'

'Yes. Not as wealthy as he is today, but his business was beginning to flourish.'

'A love marriage?'

An enigmatic smile.

'You could say so. We met in Dinard. After three weeks, he asked me if I'd consent to be his wife. My parents made inquiries.'

'Were you happy?'

He looked her in the eyes and needed no reply. He murmured the answer himself, 'There was a certain age gap. Couchet had his business. In other words, there was not a great deal of intimacy. Is that so? You ran his household. You had your life and he had his—'

'I never criticized him!' she said. 'He was a man with a great appetite for life, who needed excitement. I didn't want to hold him back.'

'Weren't you jealous?'

'At first. Then I got used to it. I believe he loved me.'

She was quite attractive, but with no spark, no spirit. Rather nondescript features. A soft body. A sober elegance. She probably made a gracious hostess, serving her friends tea in the warm, comfortable drawing room.

'Did your husband often talk to you about his first wife?'

Then her pupils contracted. She tried to hide her anger, but realized that Maigret was no fool.

'It's not for to me to—' she began.

'My apologies. Given the circumstances of his death, I'm afraid I have to be direct.'

'You don't suspect—?'

'I suspect nobody. I'm trying to piece together your husband's life, and the lives of those around him, his movements and actions during his last evening. Did you know that his ex-wife lived in the building where Couchet had his offices?'

'Yes! He told me.'

'In what terms did he talk about her?'

'He resented her . . . Then he was ashamed of his feelings and claimed that in reality she was a sad creature.'

'Why sad?'

'Because nothing could satisfy her . . . and also—'

'And also?'

'You can guess what I mean. She's very grasping. In short, she left Raymond because he didn't earn enough money. So when she found out that he was rich . . . after she'd ended up the wife of a petty bureaucrat!'

'She didn't try to—'

'No! I don't think she ever asked him for money. It's true that my husband wouldn't have told me if she had. All I know is that for him every time he bumped into her at Place des Vosges it was awkward. I think she deliberately waylaid him. She never spoke to him, but she gave him malicious looks.'

Maigret couldn't help smiling at the thought of those encounters, under the archway: Couchet getting out of the car, fresh and pink, and Madame Martin, starchy, with her black gloves, her umbrella and her handbag, her spiteful face . . .

'Is that all you know?'

'He was looking for new premises, but it's difficult to find laboratories in Paris.'

'I presume you are not aware of your husband having any enemies?'

'None! Everyone loved him. He was too kind. Kind to the point of making a fool of himself. He didn't just spend money, he threw it away. And when criticized, he'd reply that he'd spent enough years counting every *sou*, now he could afford to be generous.'

'Did he often see your family?'

'Very little! They have nothing in common, do they? And different tastes—'

Maigret found it hard to imagine Couchet in the drawing room with the young lawyer, the colonel and the stately mother.

All this made sense.

A strong, fiery, coarse young man who had started out with nothing and who had spent thirty years of his life struggling to make his fortune.

He had grown rich. In Dinard, at last he had access to a world that had hitherto been closed to him. A real young lady, a bourgeois family, tea and *petits fours*, tennis and outings to the country.

He had got married. To prove to himself that now, the world was his! To have a home like those he had only ever seen from the outside!

He had got married, too, because he was in awe of this nice, well-brought-up young lady.

And then it was the apartment on Boulevard Haussmann, with the most traditional trappings.

Except he needed outside stimulation, to see other people, talk to them without having to mind his 'P's and 'Q's . . . go to brasseries, bars . . .

And other women.

He loved his wife. He admired her. He respected her. He was in awe of her.

But precisely because he was in awe of her, he needed girls like Nine to relax with.

Madame Couchet had a question on the tip of her tongue. She was reluctant to ask it. Then she took the plunge, averting her gaze.

'I wanted to ask you if . . . It's a delicate matter . . . I'm sorry . . . He had girlfriends, I know . . . He only kept it quiet – and barely – out of consideration. I need to know whether, on that front, there'll be any problems, a scandal—'

She obviously imagined her husband's mistresses to be like prostitutes in a novel, or screen vamps!

'You have nothing to be afraid of!' smiled Maigret, who was thinking of little Nine with her distraught face and the handful of jewellery she had taken that same afternoon to the Crédit Municipal.

'There won't be any need to—?'

'No! No allowance.'

She was astonished. Perhaps a little put out, because if these women were making no demands, it must be because they were fond of her husband! And he of them.

'Have you decided on the date of the funeral?'

'My brother is dealing with it. It will take place on Thursday, at Saint-Philippe-du-Roule.'

A clatter of plates came from the dining room next door. Was the table being laid for dinner?

'All that remains is for me to thank you and take my leave. I apologize again.'

And, walking down the Boulevard Haussmann, he caught himself muttering as he filled his pipe, 'Good old Couchet!'

The words escaped his lips as if Couchet had been an old friend. And the feeling was so strong that the thought that he had only seen him dead astounded him.

He felt as if he knew him literally inside out.

Perhaps because of the three women?

First, there'd been the confectioner's daughter, in the apartment in Nanterre, despairing at the thought that her husband would never have a proper job.

Then the young lady from Dinard, and Couchet's pride and satisfaction at becoming the nephew of a colonel.

Nine . . . Their dinners at the Select . . . Hôtel Pigalle . . .

And the son who came to sponge off him! And Madame Martin who contrived to run into him under the archway, hoping perhaps to plague him with remorse.

A strange ending! All alone, in the office where he came as seldom as possible. Leaning against the half-open safe, his hands on the table.

Nobody had noticed or heard anything. The concierge, crossing the courtyard, had seen him sitting in the same place as usual behind the frosted glass, but she was mainly concerned about Madame de Saint-Marc, who was giving birth.

The madwoman upstairs had screamed! In other words, old Mathilde, padding around in felt slippers, had been concealed behind a door on the landing.

Monsieur Martin, in his putty-coloured overcoat, had come downstairs to hunt for his glove by the dustbins.

One thing was certain: right now, someone had the stolen 360,000 francs in their possession!

And someone had committed a murder!

'All men are self-centred!' Madame Martin had said bitterly, with her pained expression.

Was she the one who had the 360 brand new thousand-franc notes handed over by the Crédit Lyonnais? Did she now have money, a lot of money, a whole wad of fat notes promising years of comfort with no worries about the future or about the pension she would receive on Martin's death?

Was it Roger, with his puny body, ravaged by ether, and that Céline he'd picked up to moulder away with him in the dampness of a hotel bed?

Was it Nine, or Madame Couchet?

In any case, there was one place from which the whole thing could have been witnessed: the Martins' apartment.

And there was a woman prowling around the building, loitering in the corridors, listening at every keyhole.

'I'd better pay old Mathilde a visit!' thought Maigret.

But when he arrived at Place des Vosges the next morning, the concierge, who was sorting the post (a big pile for the Couchet laboratory and only a handful of letters for the other residents), intercepted him.

'Are you on your way up to the Martins'? I'm not sure that's a good idea. Madame Martin was taken very ill last night. We had to call the doctor out urgently. Her husband is out of his mind.'

The laboratory staff were crossing the courtyard on

their way to the offices and the lab. At a first-floor window, a manservant was shaking rugs.

A baby could be heard wailing and a nanny was crooning monotonously.

6. A Raging Fever

'Sssh! . . . She's asleep . . . Come in anyway.'

Monsieur Martin stood aside, resigned. Resigned to showing his home in a state of disorder. Resigned to showing himself ungroomed, his moustache drooping, a greenish colour, which betrayed the fact that it was dyed.

He had sat up with his wife all night. He was worn out, listless.

He tiptoed over to close the door that communicated with the bedroom, through which Maigret glimpsed the foot of the bed and a bowl on the floor.

'The concierge told you?'

He whispered, glancing anxiously at the door. As he spoke, he turned off the gas ring on which he had been making coffee.

'Some coffee?'

'No thank you. I shan't disturb you for long. I wanted to inquire after Madame Martin.'

'You're too kind!' said Martin emphatically.

He really did not suspect any ulterior motive. He was so distraught that he must have lost his critical faculties, although it was not certain he had ever possessed any.

'It's terrible, these attacks she has! Would you excuse me for drinking my coffee in front of you?'

He grew flustered on noticing that his braces were flapping against his calves. He hastily adjusted his clothes and removed the bottles of medicine that were sitting on the table.

'Does Madame Martin often suffer these attacks?'

'No. And especially not as violent as this. She's very highly strung. When she was a girl, apparently she had nervous fits every week.'

'And still does?'

Martin gave him a hangdog look, barely daring to admit, 'I have to make allowances for her. One little disagreement and she's seething!'

With his putty-coloured overcoat, carefully waxed moustache and leather gloves, he had been ridiculous. A caricature of the pretentious petty official.

But now the dye had faded from his moustache, the look in his eyes was that of a defeated man. He hadn't had the time to shave, and was still wearing his nightshirt under an old jacket.

And he cut a pathetic figure. He was, astonishingly, at least fifty-five.

'Did something upset her last night?'

'No . . . No—'

He became agitated, looking about him, panic-stricken.

'No one came to see her? Her son, for example?'

'No! You came, then we had dinner. And then—'

'What?'

'Nothing. I don't know . . . It just came over her . . . She's very sensitive. She's had so much unhappiness in her life!'

Did he really believe what he was saying? Maigret sensed that Martin was trying to convince himself.

'In short, you personally have no ideas about the murder?'

And Martin dropped the cup he was holding. Was he of a nervous disposition too?

'Why would I have any ideas? I swear . . . If I did, I . . .'

'You—'

'I don't know. It's a terrible business! Just when we're inundated at the office. I haven't even had the time to inform my boss this morning.'

He wiped his thin hand across his forehead then busied himself picking up the pieces of broken china. He spent ages looking for a cloth to clean the wooden floor.

'If only she'd listened to me, we wouldn't have stayed here.'

He was afraid, that was patent. He was beside himself with fear. But fear of what, fear of whom?

'You're a good man, aren't you, Monsieur Martin? And an honest man.'

'I have thirty-two years' service and—'

'So if you knew something that could help the police unmask the culprit, you would feel duty-bound to tell me.'

Were his teeth chattering?

'I would most definitely do so . . . but I don't know any-thing . . . and I too would like to know! This is no life . . .'

'What do you think of your stepson?'

Martin stared at Maigret in amazement.

'Roger? He's . . .'

'He's depraved, I know!'

'But he's not a bad boy, I swear. It's all his father's fault.

As my wife always says, you shouldn't give young people so much money. She's right! And as she says I don't think Couchet did it out of generosity or fatherly love, he had no interest in his son. He did it to get rid of him, to salve his conscience.'

'His conscience?'

Martin turned red, and became even more flummoxed.

'He treated Juliette badly, didn't he?' he said quietly.

'Juliette?'

'My wife, his first wife. What did he ever do for her? Nothing! He treated her like a skivvy. And she was the one who helped him through the hard times, and later—'

'He didn't give her anything, obviously. But she had remarried.'

Martin's face had turned beetroot. Maigret watched him with amazement, and pity. For he realized that the poor man was in no way to blame for this staggering story. He was merely repeating what he must have heard hundreds of times from his wife.

Couchet was rich! She was poor! And so . . .

But the civil servant was straining to listen.

'Did you not hear something?'

They kept quiet for a moment. A faint cry was heard coming from the bedroom. Martin went over and opened the door.

'What are you telling him?' asked Madame Martin.

'But . . . I—'

'It's Inspector Maigret, isn't it? . . . What does he want now?'

Maigret couldn't see her. The voice was that of someone

lying in bed, very weary, but who still has all her wits about her.

'The detective chief inspector came to inquire after you.'

'Tell him to come in. Wait! Pass me a wet towel and the mirror. And the comb.'

'You'll get yourself all upset again.'

'Hold the mirror straight, will you! No! Put it down . . . You're hopeless . . . Take away that bowl. Honestly, men! As soon as their wife's not there, the place looks like a pigsty. You can show him in now.'

Like the dining room, the bedroom was drab and cheerless, furnished in poor taste with a profusion of old curtains, old fabrics and faded rugs. The minute he stepped inside, Maigret felt Madame Martin's eyes boring into him. Her gaze was calm and extraordinarily clear.

Her drawn face broke into an invalid's syrupy smile.

'The place is a terrible mess! Please don't take any notice,' she said. 'It's because I was taken ill.'

And she stared mournfully in front of her.

'But I'm feeling better. I must be back on my feet tomorrow, for the funeral. It is tomorrow, isn't it?'

'Yes, it's tomorrow! You're prone to these attacks—'

'I had them even as a child, but my sister—'

'The sister who—?'

'I had two sisters. Now don't you go believing what's not . . . The youngest suffered fits too. She got married. Her husband turned out to be a good-for-nothing and one fine day, when she was having an attack, he had her put away. She died a week later.'

'Don't get upset!' implored Martin, who didn't know where to put himself or where to look.

'Insane?' asked Maigret.

The woman's features hardened again and there was malice in her voice.

'In other words, her husband wanted to get rid of her! Not even six months later, he married someone else. Men are all the same . . . You devote yourself, you kill yourself for them—'

'I beg you!' sighed her husband.

'I don't mean you! Although you're no better than the others.'

And Maigret suddenly sensed a whiff of hatred in the air. It was fleeting, hazy, but he was convinced he was not mistaken.

'All the same, if it weren't for me—' she went on.

Did her voice contain a threat? Her husband busied himself doing nothing. To keep up appearances, he counted out drops of a potion into a glass, one by one.

'The doctor said—'

'I don't give a fig for what the doctor said!'

'But you must . . . Here! Drink it slowly. It's not so bad.'

She looked at him, then she looked at Maigret, and finally she gave a resigned shrug and drank.

'You haven't really come to inquire after my health,' she stated suspiciously.

'I was on my way to the laboratory when the concierge told me—'

'Have you found any clues?'

'Not yet.'

She closed her eyes, to indicate fatigue. Martin looked at Maigret, who rose.

'Well, I wish you a speedy recovery. You're already much better.'

She let him leave. Maigret stopped Martin from seeing him out.

'Please, stay with your wife.'

Poor fellow! He seemed afraid to stay; it was as if he were clinging to Maigret because when there was another person there, things were not so dreadful.

'You'll see, it will turn out to be nothing serious.'

As he walked through the dining room, he heard a rustle in the corridor. And he caught up with old Mathilde just as she was about to go back into her room.

'Good morning.'

She looked at him fearfully, without replying, her hand poised on the door knob.

Maigret spoke quietly. He guessed that Madame Martin was listening; she was perfectly capable of getting out of bed to eavesdrop.

'As you probably know, I'm the detective chief inspector in charge of the investigation.'

He already sensed that he would get nothing out of the woman with her placid, moonlike face.

'What do you want from me?'

'Only to ask you if you have anything to tell me. How long have you been living here?'

'Forty years!' she replied curtly.

'You know everyone.'

'I don't talk to anyone!'

'I thought perhaps that you might have seen or heard something. Sometimes a tiny clue helps set the police on the right track.'

Someone was moving around inside the room. But the old woman kept the door determinedly shut.

'You saw nothing?'

She did not reply.

'And you heard nothing?'

'You'd do better to tell the landlord to put the gas in.'

'The gas?'

'Everyone else here has gas. But because he's not allowed to put my rent up, he refuses to install it in my room. He wants to boot me out! He's doing everything he can to force me out, but he'll be leaving before me, feet first! And you can tell him that from me.'

The door opened a tiny crack, so tiny that it seemed impossible that the fat woman could squeeze through. Then she closed it behind her and only muffled sounds came from inside the room.

'May I have your card?'

Maigret proffered his visiting card, and the butler in a striped waistcoat took it before disappearing inside the apartment, which was extraordinarily light, thanks to its five-metre-high windows. Such windows have become rare and are only found in the buildings on Place des Vosges and the Ile Saint-Louis.

The rooms were vast. From somewhere the hum of an electric vacuum cleaner could be heard. A nanny in a white uniform with a pretty blue headdress was going from one room to another. She shot the visitor an inquisitive glance.

A voice, close at hand.

'Show the detective chief inspector in.'

Monsieur de Saint-Marc was in his study, in his dressing gown, his silvery hair carefully smoothed. First he went over and closed a door, through which Maigret had the time to glimpse an antique bed, the face of a young woman on the pillow.

'Please take a seat. Naturally you want to speak to me about this terrible Couchet business.'

Despite his age, he gave an impression of health and vigour. And the atmosphere in the apartment was that of a happy home, where everything was full of light and joy.

'I was particularly saddened by this tragedy, which took place at a time of great emotion for me.'

'I am aware of that.'

There was a little glint of satisfaction in the eyes of the former ambassador. He was proud of having a child at his age.

'May I ask you to keep your voice down, as I'd rather keep this business from Madame de Saint-Marc. In her condition, it would be unfortunate . . . But what was it you wanted to ask me? I barely knew this Couchet. I'd caught a glimpse of him crossing the courtyard a couple of times. He belonged to one of the clubs I go to occasionally, the Haussmann, but he must rarely have set foot in the place. I just noticed his name in the latest directory. I believe he was quite vulgar, wasn't he?'

'In other words, he was working-class. He had struggled to become successful.'

'My wife told me he had married a woman from a very good family, a former school friend of hers. That's one of the reasons why it's better not to tell her . . . so, you wanted to ask me . . . ?'

The vast windows afforded a view of the entire Place des Vosges bathed in soft sunshine. In the square, gardeners were watering the lawns and flower beds. Drays plodded heavily past.

'Just a simple question. I know that you were on edge while your wife was in labour, which is only natural, and that several times you came down and paced up and down the courtyard. Did you meet anyone? Did you not see someone heading towards the offices at the back?'

Monsieur de Saint-Marc thought for a moment, fiddling with a paper knife.

'Wait . . . No! I don't think so. Don't forget, I had other things on my mind. The concierge would be in a better position to—'

'The concierge doesn't know anything—'

'And I . . . No! . . . Or rather . . . But it can't have anything to do with—'

'Tell me anyway.'

'At one point, I heard a noise by the dustbins. I was at a loose end, so I went over and I saw one of the residents from the second floor—'

'Madame Martin?'

'I believe that's her name. I confess, I don't know my

neighbours very well. She was rummaging in one of the zinc bins ... I remember her saying, *"One of our silver spoons must have fallen into the rubbish bin."* I asked, *"Have you found it?"* And she said, quite excitedly, *"Yes! Yes!"'*

'Then what did she do?' asked Maigret.

'She hurried back up to her apartment. She's a jittery little woman who always seems to be running ... If I recall, we lost a valuable ring in the same manner ... and the astonishing thing is that it was returned to the concierge by a rag-picker who'd found it when he was rummaging with his hook.'

'You couldn't tell me roughly what time this incident occurred?'

'That would be difficult ... Wait ... I didn't want any dinner ... But at around eight-thirty, Albert, my butler, urged me to have something and, since I refused to come to the table, he brought me some anchovy tarts in the drawing room. That was before—'

'Before eight-thirty?'

'Yes. Let us say that the incident, as you call it, took place just after eight o'clock, but I don't think it is of any significance whatsoever. What is your opinion about this business? There's a rumour going around, apparently, that the murder was committed by someone who lives here, but personally I refuse to believe it. When you think that anyone can just walk into the courtyard. By the way, I'm going to write to the landlord to request that the main door be locked at dusk.'

Maigret had risen.

'I haven't yet formed an opinion,' he said.

The concierge brought up the post and, since the door

had remained open, she suddenly caught sight of the inspector conversing with Monsieur de Saint-Marc.

Poor Madame Bourcier! She was all flustered! Her expression betrayed a world of anxieties.

Would Maigret be so bold as to suspect the Saint-Marcs? Or even simply to bother them with his questions?

'Thank you, monsieur . . . and please forgive my intrusion—'

'A cigar?'

Monsieur de Saint-Marc had the airs of a gentleman, with a tiny hint of condescending familiarity more suggestive of the politician than the diplomat.

'I am entirely at your service.'

The butler closed the door behind him. Maigret made his way slowly down the stairs and found himself in the courtyard where the delivery man from a department store was trying to find the concierge.

In the lodge, there was only a dog, a cat and the two children busy smearing milk soup all over their faces.

'Isn't your mother here?'

'She'll be back, m'sieur! She's taking the post up.'

In the ignominious corner of the courtyard, near the lodge, there were four zinc bins into which, at night, the residents came one by one to throw their household waste.

At six a.m., the concierge unlocked the main door and the municipal rubbish collectors emptied the bins into their cart.

At night, that corner was not lit up. The only light in the courtyard was on the other side, at the foot of the stairs.

What had Madame Martin come down to look for, more or less at the time when Couchet was killed?

Had she taken it into her head to look for her husband's glove?

'No!' grunted Maigret struck by a memory. Martin had only brought the rubbish down much later.

So what had she been up to? There couldn't have been a lost spoon! During the daytime, the residents are not allowed to throw anything into the dustbins.

So what were the pair of them looking for, one after the other?

Madame Martin had been rummaging in the bin itself.

Martin, on the other hand, had been looking in the area around the bins, striking matches.

And by the next morning, the glove had been found!

'Did you see the baby?' asked a voice behind Maigret.

It was the concierge, who was talking about the Saint-Marcs' child with more emotion than about her own.

'You didn't say anything to Madame, I hope? She mustn't be told—'

'I know! I know!'

'For the wreath . . . I mean the residents' wreath . . . I'm wondering whether we should have it delivered to the undertakers today or whether it's the custom only to send it to the funeral . . . The staff were very generous too, they've collected over three hundred francs.'

And, turning to the delivery man, 'What is it?'

'Saint-Marc!'

'Right-hand staircase. First floor facing. And knock gently!'

Then, to Maigret, 'You should see how many flowers

she's received! So many they don't know where to put them all. Most of them have had to be taken up to the servants' rooms. Won't you come in? Jojo! Leave your sister alone!'

The inspector was still staring at the dustbins. What on earth could the Martins have been looking for in them?

'This morning, did you put the bins out as usual?'

'No! Since I've been widowed, it's impossible! Or I'd have to take someone on, because they're much too heavy for me . . . the bin men are very kind, I give them a glass of wine from time to time and they come into the courtyard to collect them.'

'So the rag-pickers can't rummage through them!'

'Do you think so? They come into the courtyard too. Sometimes there are three or four of them, and they make an unholy mess.'

'Thank you for your help.'

And Maigret left, pondering, either forgetting or not considering it worth his while to visit the Couchet offices again as he had planned to do earlier in the day.

When he arrived at Quai des Orfèvres, he was told, 'Someone was asking for you on the telephone. A colonel.'

But he decided to pursue his hunch. Opening the door of the inspectors' office, he called out, 'Lucas! I want you to get on to this straight away. Question all the rag-pickers who operate around the Place des Vosges. If necessary, go as far as the Saint-Denis plant, where the rubbish is incinerated.'

'But—'

'We need to know if they noticed anything unusual in

the dustbins of 61, Place des Vosges, the morning before yesterday.'

He slumped in his armchair and a word came back into his mind: colonel.

What colonel? He didn't know any colonels.

Oh yes he did! There was one colonel in this case! Madame Couchet's uncle! What on earth did he want?

'Hello! Élysée 1762? This is Detective Chief Inspector Maigret from police headquarters . . . Excuse me? . . . Colonel Dormoy wants to speak to me. I'll hold the line, yes. Hello! Is that you, Colonel? . . . How? . . . A will? . . . I can't hear you very well. No, on the contrary, lower your voice! Hold the receiver a little further away. That's better. So? You have found a will that no one knew about? And not even stamped? Understood! I'll be with you in half an hour. No! There's no point my taking a taxi.'

And he lit his pipe, pushed back his armchair and crossed his legs.

7. The Three Women

'The colonel is waiting for you in Monsieur's bedroom. Please follow me.'

The room where the body had been laid out was closed. There was someone moving around next door, which must have been Madame Couchet's bedroom. The maid opened a door and Maigret glimpsed the colonel standing by the table, his hand resting lightly on it, his chin high, dignified and calm as if he were posing for a sculptor.

'Please sit down!'

Maigret ignored his invitation to sit and simply unbuttoned his heavy overcoat, placed his bowler hat on a chair and filled his pipe.

'Did you find the will yourself?' he then asked, looking about him with curiosity.

'Indeed I did, earlier today. My niece doesn't know about it yet. I have to say that it is so shocking—'

A strange bedroom, typical of Couchet! True, the furniture was period, like the rest of the apartment. There were a few items of value, but mixed in with them were things that revealed the man's vulgar tastes.

In front of the window was a table that pretty much served as his desk. On it were Turkish cigarettes and also a whole set of cheap, cherry-wood pipes which Couchet must have seasoned lovingly.

A purple dressing gown! The gaudiest he could have found! Then, at the foot of the bed, slippers with holes in their soles.

The table had a drawer.

'Note that it wasn't locked!' said the colonel. 'I don't even know if there is a key. This morning, my niece needed cash to pay a supplier and I wanted to save her the trouble of writing a cheque. I searched this room, and this is what I came across.'

An envelope with the Grand-Hôtel crest. Pale blue notepaper with the same letterhead.

Then a few lines that appeared to have been written distractedly, like a rough draft.

This is my last will and testament . . .

And further down, these surprising words:

Since I shall probably not get around to finding out about inheritance law, I instruct my lawyer, Maître Dampierre, to do his utmost to ensure that my fortune is shared as equally as possible between:

1 My wife Germaine, née Dormoy;

2 My first wife, now Madame Martin, residing at 61, Place des Vosges;

3 Nine Moinard, residing at Hôtel Pigalle, Rue Pigalle.

'What do you make of that?'

Maigret was jubilant. This will endeared Couchet to him even further.

'Naturally,' continued the colonel, 'this will does not hold water. There are numerous reasons why it would be deemed null and void and, immediately after the funeral, we intend to contest it. But the reason I felt it was useful and urgent to discuss it with you is that—'

Maigret was still smiling, as if he had witnessed a good prank. Even the Grand-Hôtel letterhead! Like many businessmen, Couchet probably held some of his meetings there. So, while waiting for someone, probably, in the lobby or the smoking room, he had picked up a blotter and scribbled those few lines.

He hadn't sealed the envelope! He'd stuffed the whole thing in his drawer, postponing the business of having a proper will drawn up.

That had been two weeks ago.

'You must have been struck by one outrageous detail,' the colonel was saying. 'Couchet simply doesn't mention his son! That alone is enough to render the will null and void and—'

'Do you know Roger?'

'Me? . . . No.'

And Maigret was still smiling.

'I was saying earlier that if I asked you to come here, it was because—'

'Do you know Nine Moinard?'

The poor man jumped as if someone had stepped on his toe.

'I don't need to know her. Her address alone, Rue Pigalle, gives me an idea of . . . Now what was I saying? . . . Oh yes! Did you notice the date on the will? It is recent! Couchet died two weeks after writing it. He was murdered! Now imagine that one of the two women concerned was aware of these provisions . . . I have every reason to believe that neither of them is rich.'

'Why two women?'

'What do you mean?'

'Three women! The will names three women! Couchet's three women, if you like!'

The colonel assumed that Maigret was joking.

'I was being serious,' he said. 'Don't forget that there is a dead man in the house. And that this affects the future of several people.'

Of course. All the same, Maigret felt like laughing. He himself couldn't have said why.

'Thank you for letting me know.'

The colonel was vexed. He could not understand this attitude on the part of a police inspector of Maigret's senior rank.

'I suppose—'

'Goodbye, Colonel. Kindly pay my respects to Madame Couchet.'

In the street, he couldn't help muttering, 'Good old Couchet!'

Coldly, just like that, in complete seriousness, he had put his three women in his will! Including his first wife, now Madame Martin, who was constantly appearing in front of him with her contemptuous gaze, like a living reproof! Including courageous little Nine, who did everything she could to entertain him.

On the other hand, he had forgotten that he had a son!

For a good few minutes, Maigret wondered whom to tell first. Madame Martin, who would probably leap out of her bed at the news of a fortune? Or Nine?

'But they haven't got their hands on the cash yet.'

This business could go on for years! The family would contest the will. Madame Martin, in any case, wouldn't allow them to push her around.

'Even so, the colonel has been honest. He could have burned the will and no one would ever have known.'

And a light-hearted Maigret crossed the Europe district on foot. A wan sun gave out a little warmth and there was joy in the air.

'Good old Couchet!'

He entered the lift of Hôtel Pigalle without announcing himself and a few moments later he was knocking at Nine's door. He heard footsteps inside the room. The door opened a fraction, just enough for a hand to poke through. The hand remained dangling in the air.

A woman's hand, already wrinkled. Since Maigret didn't respond, the hand grew impatient and the face of an elderly Englishwoman appeared. She launched into an unintelligible tirade.

Or rather, Maigret guessed that the Englishwoman was expecting her post, which explained the outstretched hand. What was clear was that Nine no longer occupied her room and that she probably didn't live in the hotel any more.

'Too expensive for her,' he thought.

And he paused uncertainly outside the neighbouring door. A valet decided him, asking him suspiciously, 'Can I help you?'

'Monsieur Couchet—'

'Is he not answering?'

'I haven't knocked yet.'

And Maigret was still smiling. He was in a buoyant mood. That morning, he suddenly felt as if he were playing a part in a farce. Life itself was a farce! Couchet's death was a farce, especially his will!

'. . . C'min!'

The bolt slid back. The first thing Maigret did was to march over and draw the curtains and open the window.

Céline had not even woken up. Roger rubbed his eyes and yawned, 'Oh! It's you.'

There was an improvement: the room didn't reek of ether. The clothes were in a heap on the floor.

'. . . What d'you want?'

Roger sat up in bed, picked up the glass of water from his bedside table and drained it in one go.

'The will has been found!' announced Maigret covering up a naked thigh belonging to Céline, who was lying curled up.

'So what?'

Roger showed no excitement. Barely a vague curiosity.

'So what? It's a strange will! It will certainly cause much ink to flow and earn the lawyers a lot of money. Can you imagine, your father has left his entire fortune to his three women!'

The young man struggled to understand.

'His three . . . ?'

'Yes! His current lawful wife. Then your mother! And lastly his girlfriend Nine, who was living in the room next door till yesterday! He has instructed the lawyer to ensure they each receive an equal share.'

Roger didn't bat an eyelid. He appeared to be thinking. But not to be thinking about something that concerned him personally.

'That's priceless!' he said at length in a serious tone that belied his words.

'That's exactly what I said to the colonel.'

'What colonel?'

'An uncle of Madame Couchet's. He's playing the head of the family.'

'I bet he's not happy!'

'Too right!'

The young man thrust his legs out of the bed and grabbed a pair of trousers draped over the back of a chair.

'You don't seem particularly bothered by this news.'

'Oh me, you know . . .'

He buttoned up his trousers, looked for a comb and closed the window, which was letting in the cold air.

'Don't you need money?'

Maigret was suddenly solemn. His gaze became probing, questioning.

'I don't know.'

'You don't know whether you need money?'

Roger darted Maigret a shifty look and Maigret felt ill at ease.

'I don't give a — !'

'It's not as if you are earning a good living.'

'I don't earn a bean!'

He yawned and looked mournfully at his reflection in the mirror. Maigret noticed that Céline had woken up. She didn't move. She must have overheard some of the conversation, for she was watching the two men with curiosity.

She too needed the glass of water! And the atmosphere in that untidy room, with its stale smell, those two listless beings, was the quintessence of a dispirited world.

'Do you have any savings?'

Roger was beginning to tire of this conversation. He looked around for his jacket, took out a slim wallet embossed with his initials and threw it to Maigret.

'Have a look!'

Two 100-franc notes, a few smaller ones, a driving licence and an old cloakroom ticket.

'What do you intend to do if you are deprived of your inheritance?'

'I don't want any inheritance!'

'You won't contest the will?'

'No!'

That was strange. Maigret, who had been staring at the carpet, looked up.

'Three hundred and sixty thousand francs are enough for you?'

Then the young man's attitude changed. He walked over to the inspector, stopped within inches of him, at the point where their shoulders were touching. And, his fists clenched, he snarled, 'Say that again!'

At that moment, there was something thuggish about him, A coarse air, the scent of the café brawl.

'I'm asking you if Couchet's 360,000 francs are—'

He just managed to grab Roger's arm in mid-air. Otherwise he would have received one of the biggest punches of his life!

'Calm down!'

But Roger was calm! He wasn't struggling! He was pale. He stared fixedly. He was waiting until the inspector was prepared to release him.

Was it to strike again? Meanwhile, Céline had jumped out of bed, despite being half-naked. Maigret could sense she was about to open the door to call for help.

Everything happened peacefully. Maigret only held on to Roger's wrist for a few seconds, and when he gave him back his freedom of movement, the young man did not move.

There was a long silence. It was as if each one of them was afraid to break it, the way, in a fight, each opponent is reluctant to deliver the first punch.

Finally it was Roger who spoke.

'You've got to be kidding!'

He picked up a mauve dressing gown from the floor and threw it over to his companion.

'Do you want to tell me what you plan to do, once you've spent your 200 francs?'

'What have I done until now?'

'There's just one little difference: your father's dead and you can no longer sponge off him.'

Roger shrugged as if to say that Maigret had got the wrong end of the stick.

There was an indefinable atmosphere, not exactly of drama, but something else – a poignancy perhaps, a bohemian atmosphere but devoid of poetry. Perhaps it was the sight of the wallet and the two 100-franc notes? Or was it the anxious woman, who had just realized that tomorrow would not be like the previous days, that she'd have to find a new source of support?

But no! It was Roger himself who was frightening. Because his behaviour and actions were out of character, contradicting what Maigret knew of his past.

His calmness . . . and it wasn't an act! He was truly calm, calm like someone who—

'Give me your gun!' suddenly commanded the chief inspector.

The young man pulled it out of his trouser pocket and proffered it with the ghost of a smile.

'Promise me you'll—'

He stopped in mid-sentence when he saw the woman about to scream in terror. She couldn't grasp what was going on, but she knew it was something very bad.

Irony, in Roger's eyes.

Maigret almost ran out of the room. Having nothing further to say, no gesture to make, he beat a retreat, banging into the door frame on his way out and stifling a curse.

Back in the street, his cheery mood of that morning had dissipated. He no longer found life a joke. He looked up at the couple's window. It was closed. You couldn't see a thing.

He was uneasy, as one is when nothing makes sense any more.

Roger had given him two or three looks . . . He couldn't have explained it, but they were not the looks he was expecting. They were looks that were somehow at odds with the rest.

He retraced his steps, because he had forgotten to ask at the hotel for Nine's new address.

'Don't know!' said the porter. 'She paid for her room and left carrying her suitcase! Didn't need a taxi. She must have gone to the cheapest hotel around here.'

'Look, if . . . if anything were to happen here . . . Yes . . . something unexpected . . . would you kindly inform me personally at police headquarters? Detective Chief Inspector Maigret.'

He was annoyed at himself for having said that. What could happen? Even so he recalled the two 100-franc notes in Roger's wallet and Céline's look of fear.

A quarter of an hour later, he entered the Moulin Bleu via the stage door. The auditorium was empty, dark, the seats and the sides of the boxes covered in glossy green silk fabric.

On the stage, six women, shivering despite their coats, were repeatedly rehearsing the same step – 'a ridiculously easy step' – while a short, pudgy man bellowed a tune at the top of his lungs.

'One! . . . Two! . . . Tra la la la . . . No! . . . Tra la la la . . . Three! . . . Three, for heaven's sake!'

Nine was the second woman in the line. She recognized

Maigret, who was standing by a column. The man had spotted him too, but he wasn't bothered.

'One! . . . Two! . . . Tra la la—'

It went on for fifteen minutes. It was colder in here than outside and Maigret's feet were frozen. At last the squat man wiped his forehead and cursed his dancers by way of a farewell.

'Come to see me?' he yelled at Maigret from a distance.

'No! . . . I've come to see—'

Nine walked over, embarrassed, wondering whether she should hold out her hand to the inspector.

'I have some important news for you—'

'Not here . . . We're not allowed to have visitors at the theatre . . . Except in the evenings, because they have to pay.'

They sat at a pedestal table in a little bar next door.

'They've found Couchet's will. He left his fortune to three women.'

She looked at him in amazement, without suspecting the truth.

'First of all, his first wife, even though she's remarried, then his second wife . . . And then you.'

She continued to stare at Maigret, who saw her pupils dilate and then mist over.

And finally she buried her face in her hands to cry.

8. *The Home Nurse*

'He had heart disease. He knew it.'

Nine sipped her ruby-coloured aperitif.

'That's why he took things easy. He said he'd worked enough, that it was time for him to enjoy life.'

'Did he sometimes talk about death?'

'Often! But not . . . not that kind of death! He was thinking of his heart disease.'

They were in one of those little bars where all the customers are regulars. The owner watched Maigret covertly as if he were a bourgeois meeting his mistress. At the counter, the men were talking about the afternoon's racing.

'Was he sad?'

'It's hard to explain! Because he wasn't like other men. For example, when we were at the theatre, or somewhere else, he'd be enjoying himself. Then, for no reason, he'd say with a deep laugh, *"Life's a bitch, isn't it, Ninette!"*'

'Did he take care of his son?'

'No.'

'Did he talk about him?'

'Almost never! Only when he came to scrounge.'

'And what did he say?'

'He'd sigh, *"What a stupid idiot!"*'

Maigret had already intuited that, for one reason or another, Couchet had little affection for his son. It even seemed as if he was disgusted by the young man. Disgusted to the point of not trying to come to his rescue!

For he had never lectured him. And he gave him money to get rid of him, or out of pity.

'Waiter! How much do I owe you?'

'Four francs sixty!'

Nine left the bar with him and they stood on the pavement of Rue Fontaine for a moment.

'Where are you living now?'

'Rue Lepic, the first hotel on the left. I haven't even looked at the name yet. It's fairly clean.'

'When you're rich you'll be able—'

She gave him a watery smile.

'You know very well I'll never be rich! I'm not the sort for all that.'

The strangest thing was that Maigret had that very impression. Nine didn't look like someone who would be rich one day. He couldn't have said why.

'I'll accompany you to Place Pigalle, where I'm going to get my tram.'

They walked slowly, Maigret huge, burly, and Nine petite next to his broad back.

'If you knew how lost I feel being on my own! Luckily there's the theatre, with two rehearsals a day until the show opens.'

She had to take two steps to each of Maigret's strides, and was almost running. At the corner of Rue Pigalle, she stopped abruptly, while the inspector frowned and muttered under his breath, 'The fool!'

But they couldn't see anything. Opposite Hôtel Pigalle, around forty people were gathered. A police officer stood in the doorway trying to move them on.

That was all, but there was that particular atmosphere, that silence that you only encounter in the street when a tragedy occurs.

'What's going on?' stammered Nine. 'In my hotel!'

'No! It's nothing! Go back to your room—'

'But . . . something—'

'Go!' he snapped.

And she obeyed, scared, while Maigret elbowed his way through the crowd. He charged like a ram. Women shouted abuse at him. The police sergeant recognized him and asked him to step inside the hotel.

The district detective chief inspector was already there, talking to the porter, who cried out, pointing at Maigret, 'It's him! I recognize him—'

The two inspectors shook hands. From the little lounge that opened off the lobby, sobs, groans and indistinct murmurs could be heard.

'How did he do it?' asked Maigret.

'The girl who lives with him states that he was standing by the window, very calm. She got dressed, and he watched her, whistling. He only paused to tell her she had lovely thighs, but that her calves were too thin. Then he started whistling again, and suddenly everything went quiet. She felt a terrible emptiness . . . He was no longer there! He couldn't have left via the door.'

'Got it! Did he injure anyone as he landed on the pavement?'

'No one. Killed outright. Spine broken in two places.'

'Here's the ambulance,' announced the sergeant coming over to them.

And the district detective chief inspector explained to Maigret, 'There's nothing more to be done. Do you know whether he has any family who need to be informed? When you arrived, the porter was just telling me that the young man had had a visitor this morning . . . a tall, well-built man. He was giving me a description of this man when you turned up. It was you! Should I write a report anyway, or will you deal with everything?'

'Write a report.'

'What about the family?'

'I'll deal with them.'

He opened the door to the lounge, saw a shape lying on the floor, completely covered with a blanket from one of the beds.

Céline, crumpled in an armchair, was now making a regular wailing noise, while a plump woman – the owner or the manager – was trying to comfort her.

'It's not as if he killed himself for you, is it? It's not your fault, you never refused him anything.'

Maigret did not lift up the blanket, did not even make Céline aware of his presence.

A few moments later, the body was carried out to the ambulance, which set off in the direction of the mortuary.

Then, gradually, the crowd in Rue Pigalle dispersed. The

last stragglers didn't even know whether there had been a fire, a suicide or the arrest of a pickpocket.

He was whistling . . . and suddenly everything went quiet.

Slowly, slowly Maigret climbed the staircase of the Place des Vosges and, as he reached the second floor, he scowled.

Old Mathilde's door was ajar. She was probably lurking behind it, spying. But he shrugged and pulled the bell cord by the Martins' front door.

He had his pipe in his mouth. For a second he considered putting it in his pocket, then, once again, he shrugged.

The sound of bottles clinking. A vague murmur. Two male voices coming closer and at last the door opened.

'Very good, doctor . . . Yes, doctor . . . Thank you, doctor.'

A crushed Monsieur Martin, who had not yet had time to get dressed and whom Maigret found in the same sorry get-up as that morning.

'It's you?'

The doctor headed for the staircase while Monsieur Martin showed the inspector in, glancing furtively in the direction of the bedroom.

'Is she worse?'

'We don't know . . . The doctor won't say . . . He'll be back this evening.'

He picked up a prescription that was lying on top of the wireless, and stared at it with vacant eyes.

'I don't even have anyone to send to the pharmacy!'

'What happened?'

'More or less the same as last night, but more violent.

She began shivering, mumbling incoherently . . . I sent for the doctor and he tells me she has a temperature of nearly forty.'

'Is she delirious?'

'You can't understand anything she says, I tell you! We need ice and a rubber pouch to place on her forehead.'

'Do you want me to stay here while you go to the pharmacy?'

Monsieur Martin was about to say no, then he resigned himself.

He put on an overcoat and left, gesticulating, a tragic and grotesque figure, and then came back because he had forgotten to take any money.

Maigret had no ulterior motive for remaining in the apartment. He showed no interest in anything, didn't open a single drawer, didn't even glance at a pile of correspondence sitting on a table.

He could hear the patient's irregular breathing. From time to time she gave a long sigh, then babbled a jumble of syllables.

When Monsieur Martin came back, he found him in the same spot.

'Have you got everything you need?'

'Yes . . . This is terrible! . . . And I haven't even let my office know!'

Maigret helped him break up the ice and put it in a red rubber pouch.

'And yet you didn't have any visitors this morning?'

'Nobody . . .'

'And you didn't receive any letters?'

'Nothing . . . Circulars.'

Madame Martin's forehead was perspiring and her greying hair was plastered to her temples. Her lips were pale, but her eyes remained extraordinarily alert.

Did they recognize Maigret, who was holding the ice-filled pouch on her forehead?

It was impossible to say. But she seemed to have quietened down a little. She lay still with the red pouch on her forehead, staring at the ceiling.

The inspector led Monsieur Martin into the dining room.

'I've got several pieces of news for you.'

'Oh!' he said with a shiver of anxiety.

'Couchet's will has been found. He has left a third of his fortune to your wife.'

'What?'

And the civil servant floundered, panic-stricken, overwhelmed by this news.

'You say he's left us . . . ?'

'A third of his fortune! It's likely that things won't be straightforward. His second wife will probably contest the will. Because she only receives a third, too. The last third goes to another person, Couchet's most recent mistress, a certain Nine—'

Why did Martin seem so crestfallen? Worse than crestfallen, devastated! As if his arms and legs had been severed! He stared fixedly at the floor, unable to regain his composure.

'The second piece of news is not so good. It concerns your stepson—'

'Roger?'

'He committed suicide this morning, by jumping out of the window of his room in Rue Pigalle.'

Then he saw the petty official's hackles rise, as he shot him a look of anger, of rage, and shouted, 'What are you telling me? You're trying to drive me mad, aren't you? Admit that all this is a trick to get me to talk!'

'Not so loud! Your wife—'

'I don't care! You're lying! It isn't possible.'

He was unrecognizable. In one fell swoop his shyness, the good manners that were of such importance to him had all deserted him.

It was strange to see his face distraught, his lips quivering and his hands waving around in mid-air.

'I swear to you,' said Maigret, 'that both items of news are official.'

'But why would he have done that? I tell you, it's enough to drive a person insane! Actually, that's what's happening! My wife is going mad! You've seen her! And if this goes on, I'll end up going mad, too. We'll all go mad!'

His eyes were darting around wildly. He had lost all self-control.

'Her son jumping out of the window! And the will—'

His features were tense and suddenly he burst into tears – it was tragic, comical, horrible.

'Please! Do calm down—'

'An entire lifetime . . . Thirty-two years . . . Every day . . . At nine o'clock . . . Never a foot wrong . . . All that for—'

'Please . . . Remember your wife can hear you, and that she's very unwell—'

'What about me? Do you think I'm not unwell too? Do you think I could stand such a life for long?'

He didn't look the sort to cry, and that made his tears all the more poignant.

'It's nothing to do with you, is it? He's only your stepson. He's not your responsibility.'

Martin looked at the chief inspector, suddenly calm, but not for long.

'He's not my responsibility—'

He flew off the handle.

'Even so, I'm the one who has to deal with all the trouble! You dare to come here telling these stories! On the stairs, the residents give me strange looks. And I bet they suspect me of killing that Couchet! Absolutely! And, anyway, how do I know you don't suspect me as well? What do you want with us? Huh! Huh! You don't answer! You wouldn't dare answer. People choose the weakest! A man who's unable to defend himself . . . And my wife is sick . . . And—'

As he gesticulated, he banged the wireless with his elbow. It wobbled and crashed on to the floor amid a tinkle of broken bulbs.

Then the petty official resurfaced.

'That wireless cost twelve hundred francs! . . . I saved up for three years to buy it.'

A groan came from the bedroom next door. He listened out, but didn't move.

'Does your wife need anything?'

It was Maigret who put his head inside the bedroom. Madame Martin was still in bed. The inspector met her gaze and would have been unable to say whether it was a look of acute intelligence or one clouded by fever.

She did not attempt to speak, but let him go.

In the dining room, Martin was resting both elbows on a dresser, holding his head in his hands and staring at the wallpaper, a few centimetres from his face.

'Why would he kill himself?'

'Suppose for example that it was he who—'

Silence. A crackling. A strong smell of burning. Martin hadn't noticed.

'Is there something on the stove?' asked Maigret.

He went into the kitchen, blue with steam. On the gas ring he found a milk pan whose contents had boiled over and which was about to explode. He turned off the gas, opened the window and caught a glimpse of the court-yard, Doctor Rivière's Serums laboratory, the director's car parked in front of the porch. And he could hear the clatter of typewriters in the offices.

If Maigret was lingering, it was not without a reason. He wanted to give Martin the time to calm down, even to decide on an attitude to adopt. He slowly filled his pipe and lit it with an igniter hanging above the gas stove.

When he came back into the dining room, the man had not budged, but he was calmer. He straightened up with a sigh, fumbled for a handkerchief and blew his nose loudly.

'All this is going to end badly, isn't it?' he began.

'There are already two dead!' replied Maigret.

'Two dead.'

An effort. An effort that must have been extremely harrowing, but Martin, who was about to get all agitated again, managed to remain composed.

'In that case, I think it would be best—'

'That it would be best . . .?'

Maigret barely dared speak. He held his breath. He felt a pang in his chest, for he sensed he was close to the truth.

'Yes,' groaned Martin to himself. 'Too bad! It's essential . . . ess-en-tial—'

But then he walked automatically over to the door of the bedroom, and looked deep into the room.

Maigret was still waiting, motionless, not saying a word.

Martin said nothing. His wife remained silent. But something must have been happening.

The situation dragged on and on. The inspector was growing impatient.

'Well?'

Martin turned slowly towards him, with a different face.

'What?'

'You were saying that—'

Monsieur Martin tried to smile.

'That what?'

'That it was best, to avert any further tragedies—'

'That it was best to what?'

He wiped his hand across his forehead, like someone finding it difficult to remember.

'Please forgive me! I'm so distraught—'

'That you have forgotten what you wanted to say?'

'Yes . . . I don't remember . . . Look! . . . She's asleep.'

He pointed to Madame Martin, who had closed her eyes

and whose face had turned purple, probably from the ice being applied to her forehead.

'What do you know?' asked Maigret in the tone he used for smart-aleck prisoners.

'Me?'

And from then on, all his answers were in that vein! What's known as acting dumb. Repeating a word in astonishment.

'You were on the point of telling me the truth—'

'The truth?'

'Come on! Don't try and pretend you're an idiot. You know who killed Couchet.'

'Me? . . . I know?'

If he had never been given a clout, he was within a whisker of receiving an almighty one from Maigret's hand!

Maigret, his jaws clenched, watched the unmoving woman who was asleep, or pretending to be, then the man whose eyelids were still puffy from the previous outburst, his features drawn, his moustache drooping.

'Will you take responsibility for what might happen?'

'What might happen?'

'You're wrong, Martin!'

'Wrong how?'

What was going on? For a minute, perhaps, the man who had been about to speak had stood between the two rooms, his eyes riveted on his wife's bed. Maigret had not heard a sound. Martin had not moved.

Now she was asleep, and he was feigning innocence!

'Forgive me . . . I think there are moments when I don't

know what I'm saying . . . Admit that a person can go mad if—'

All the same, he remained sad, lugubrious even. He had the attitude of a condemned man. His gaze avoided Maigret's face, fluttered over familiar objects and finally settled on the wireless set, which he proceeded to pick up, crouched on the floor, his back to the inspector.

'What time will the doctor be coming?'

'I don't know. He said "this evening".'

Maigret left, slamming the door behind him. He found himself nose-to-nose with old Mathilde, who got such a fright that she stood transfixed, her mouth open.

'You haven't anything to tell me either, have you? . . . Eh? . . . Perhaps you're going to claim you don't know anything either?'

She tried to compose herself. She had both hands beneath her apron in the classic pose of an elderly house-wife.

'Come and let's go back to your room.'

Her felt slippers glided over the floorboards. She paused, reluctant to push her half-open door.

'Go on, go inside.'

And Maigret followed her in, kicked the door shut, not even sparing a glance for the madwoman sitting by the window.

'Now, talk! Understood?'

And he sank with his full weight on to a chair.

9. The Man with the Pension

'First of all, they spend their whole time arguing!'

Maigret didn't bat an eyelid. He was up to his ears in all this day-to-day unpleasantness, which was more repulsive than the murder itself.

The old woman before him had a malevolent expression of jubilation and menace. She was talking! She was going to talk some more! Out of hatred for the Martins, for the dead man, for all the residents of the building, out of hatred for the whole of humanity! And out of hatred for Maigret!

She remained standing, her hands clasped over her soft, fat belly, and it was as though she had been waiting for this moment all her life.

It was not a smile that hovered on her lips. It was bliss that melted her!

'*First of all*, they spend their whole time arguing.'

She had time. She distilled her words. She allowed herself the leisure of expressing her contempt for people who argue.

'Worse than ragamuffins! It's always been like that! I sometimes wonder how he's managed not to wring her neck yet.'

'Ah! You were expecting . . .?'

'When you live in a place like this, you have to expect anything . . .'

She placed careful emphasis on her words. Was she more loathsome than ridiculous or more ridiculous than loathsome?

The room was large. There was an unmade bed with grey sheets that can never have been hung out to dry in the open air. A table, an old wardrobe, a stove.

The madwoman sat in an armchair staring in front of her with a gentle half-smile.

'Do you ever have visitors, may I ask?' said Maigret.

'Never!'

'And your sister never leaves this room?'

'Sometimes, she gets out on to the staircase.'

A depressing drabness. A smell of unsavoury poverty, of old age, of death even?

'Mind you, it's always the wife who goes for him!'

Maigret barely had the energy to question her. He vaguely looked at her. He was listening.

'Over money matters, of course! Not over women . . . Although once she suspected, when she did the accounts, that he had visited a house of ill-repute, and she gave him a hard time.'

'Does she hit him?'

Maigret spoke without irony. The idea was no more preposterous than any other. There were so many implausibilities that nothing would be surprising.

'I don't know if she hits him, but in any case she smashes plates . . . Then she cries, saying that she'll never have a happy marriage.'

'In other words, there are scenes almost every day?'

'Not big scenes! But carping. Two or three big scenes a week.'

'That must keep you busy!'

She wasn't sure she had understood and began to look slightly anxious.

'What does she complain about most often?'

'"When you can't afford to feed a wife, you don't marry!

'"You don't deceive a woman telling her you'll be getting a rise when it's not true.

'"You don't steal a wife from a man like Couchet, who's capable of earning millions.

'"Civil servants are cowards. You should work for yourself, be prepared to take risks, be entrepreneurial, if you want to get anywhere."'

Poor Martin, with his gloves, his putty-coloured overcoat and his waxed moustache! Maigret could imagine the hail of criticism she constantly rained on him.

But he had done his best! Couchet before him had been subjected to the same criticisms, and she must have said to him, 'Look at Monsieur Martin! Now there's a clever man! And he hopes to have a wife one day! She'll get a pension if anything happens to him! Whereas you—'

All this sounded like a sinister accusation. Madame Martin had been wrong, had been wronged, had wronged everyone!

There was a terrible mistake at the root of all this!

The confectioner's daughter from Meaux wanted money. That was an established fact. It was a necessity!

She felt it. She was born to have money, and consequently, it was up to her husband to earn it!

But Couchet didn't earn enough. And she wouldn't even be entitled to a pension if he died.

So she had married Martin.

Except that it was Couchet who had become a millionaire, when it was too late! And there was no way of giving Martin wings, no way to convince him to leave the Registry Office and to sell serums too, or something that would bring in money.

She was unhappy. She had always been unhappy. Life seemed determined to cheat her cruelly!

Old Mathilde's glaucous eyes stared at Maigret, making him think of jellyfish.

'Did her son ever visit her?'

'Sometimes.'

'Did she quarrel with him too?'

This was Mathilde's big moment! She took her time. After all, she had all the time in the world!

'She used to advise him: *"Your father's rich! He should be ashamed of himself, not getting you a better job! You don't even have a car . . . and do you know why? Because of that woman who married him for his money! Because that's the only reason she married him!*

'"*And God knows what she's got in store for you later . . . Will you even get a share of the fortune that should be yours?*

'"*That's why you should get money out of him now, put it away in a safe place. I'll look after it for you if you like. Do you want me to look after it for you?"*'

And Maigret, gazing at the filthy floor, thought hard, his forehead furrowed.

He concluded that among this hodgepodge of sentiments he could identify one overriding feeling which had perhaps led to all the others: anxiety! A morbid, pathological anxiety verging on madness.

Madame Martin always talked about what might happen: her husband's death, poverty if he didn't leave her a pension . . . She was afraid for her son!

It was a nightmare, an obsession.

'What did Roger reply?'

'Nothing! He never stayed long! He must have had better things to do elsewhere.'

'Did he come the day of the murder?'

'I don't know.'

And the madwoman in her corner, as old as Mathilde, still gazed at the inspector, smiling her blissful smile.

'Did the Martins have a conversation that was more interesting than usual?'

'I don't know.'

'Did Madame Martin go downstairs at around eight o'clock in the evening?'

'I don't remember! I can't be in the corridor all the time.'

Was it thoughtlessness, transcendent irony? In any case, she was holding something back. Maigret could tell. Not all the pus had come out.

'That evening, they had an argument.'

'Why?'

'I don't know.'

'Weren't you listening?'

She did not reply. Her expression signified: 'That's my business!'

'What else do you know?'

'I know why she's ill!'

And that was her trump card. Her hands trembled, still clasped over her stomach. This was the high point of her entire career.

'Why?'

The moment needed savouring.

'Because . . . Wait a minute, let me ask my sister if she needs anything . . . Fanny, are you thirsty? . . . Hungry? . . . Not too hot?'

The little cast-iron stove was red hot. The old woman floated around the room, gliding soundlessly across the floor in her felt slippers.

'Because?'

'Because he didn't bring home the money!'

She spelled out this sentence and then clammed up once and for all. It was over! She would not say another word. She had said enough.

'What money?'

A waste of time! She wouldn't answer any more questions.

'It's none of my business! That's what I heard! Make of it what you will . . . Now, I have to see to my sister.'

He left, leaving the two old women to heaven-knows-what routine.

He was all churned up. His stomach heaved, as in sea-sickness. *He didn't bring home the money . . .*

Was there not an explanation? Martin decided to rob

the first husband, perhaps to stop her from criticizing his mediocrity. She watched him out of the window. He left the office with the 360 notes . . .

Except that, when he came back, he no longer had them! Had he hidden them somewhere safe? Had he been robbed in turn? Or had he become scared and got rid of the money by throwing it into the Seine?

Was mediocre Monsieur Martin in his putty-coloured overcoat a killer?

Earlier on, he had wanted to talk. His weariness was that of a guilty man who no longer has the strength to keep quiet, who prefers immediate prison to the anguish of waiting.

But why was his wife the one who was ill?

And above all, why was it Roger who had killed himself?

Was all this perhaps a figment of Maigret's imagination? Why not suspect Nine, or Madame Couchet, or even the colonel?

Making his way slowly down the stairs, the inspector met Monsieur de Saint-Marc, who turned around.

'Oh! It's you.'

He extended a condescending hand.

'Any news? Do you think you'll get to the bottom of it all?'

Then came the scream of the madwoman upstairs, who must have been abandoned by her sister, gone to stand guard behind some door.

A lovely funeral. A big turnout. Distinguished people. Especially Madame Couchet's family and their neighbours on Boulevard Haussmann.

Only Couchet's sister in the front row looked out of place, even though she had gone to impossible lengths to be elegant. She was crying. Above all, she had a noisy way of blowing her nose that prompted the dead man's mother-in-law to glare at her every time.

Immediately behind the family sat the laboratory staff.

And, with the employees, old Mathilde, very dignified, sure of herself, sure of her right to be there.

The black dress she wore must have served for just that purpose: attending funerals! Her eyes met Maigret's, and she deigned to give him a slight nod.

The singing, accompanied by the organ, burst forth, the cantor's bass, the deacon's falsetto: *Et ne nos inducas in tentationem . . .*

The scraping of chairs. The catafalque was high, and yet it was invisible beneath all the flowers and wreaths.

The residents of 61, Place des Vosges

Mathilde must have given her share. Had the Martins added their names to the list of contributors too?

Madame Martin was not there. She was still in bed.

Libera nos, domine . . .

The absolution. The end. The master of ceremonies slowly leading the procession. Maigret, in a corner, by a confessional box, came across Nine, whose little nose was all red. She hadn't bothered to give it a dab of powder.

'It's terrible, isn't it?' she said.

'What's terrible?'

'Everything! I don't know! That music . . . and that smell of chrysanthemums.'

She bit her lower lip to stifle a sob.

'You know . . . I've thought a lot about . . . Well, I sometimes think he suspected something.'

'Are you going to the cemetery?'

'What do you think? People might see me, mightn't they? Perhaps it's better if I don't go . . . Even though I'd so like to know where they put him.'

'You can always ask the keeper.'

'True.'

They were whispering. The footsteps of the last of the guests died away on the other side of the door. Cars started up.

'You were saying that he suspected something?'

'Perhaps not that he would die in that manner . . . but he knew he didn't have long. He had quite a serious heart disease.'

Maigret could sense that she had been fretting, that for hours and hours on end a single question had been on her mind.

'Something he said came back to me.'

'Was he afraid?'

'No! On the contrary. When anyone happened to mention cemeteries, he would laugh and say, *"The only place where you'll find peace and quiet . . . A nice little corner in Père-Lachaise."*'

'Did he joke a lot?'

'Especially when he wasn't happy . . . Does that make

sense? He didn't like to show he was worried. At those times, he tried somehow to snap out of it, to find something to laugh about.'

'When he spoke of his first wife, for example?'

'He never talked to me about her.'

'What about his second wife?'

'No! He didn't talk about anyone in particular . . . He would talk about people in general . . . He found they were strange creatures. If a waiter cheated him, he would look at him more affectionately than the others. *"A rascal!"* he would say. And he'd say it in an amused tone, pleased even!'

It was cold. A real November day. Maigret and Nine had no business in this district of Saint-Philippe-du-Roule.

'Is everything all right at the Moulin Bleu?'

'It's fine!'

'I'll come by and say hello one evening.'

Maigret shook her hand, and jumped on to the platform of an omnibus.

He needed to be alone, to think, or rather to let his mind wander. He pictured the procession arriving soon at the cemetery . . . Madame Couchet, the colonel, the brother, the people who must be gossiping about the strange will . . .

What had the Martins been up to, rummaging around the bins?

For that was the crux of the story. Martin had poked around the dustbins claiming he was looking for a glove, which he hadn't found but had been wearing the next morning. Madame Martin had also rifled through the rubbish, talking of a silver spoon thrown out accidentally.

'. . . *because he didn't bring home the money*,' old Mathilde had said.

In fact, things must have been lively at that hour in Place des Vosges! The madwoman, who must be on her own, wouldn't she be screaming as usual?

The omnibus was full, and drove past bus stops without stopping. A man, pressed up against Maigret, was saying to his neighbour, 'Did you read about that business with the thousand-franc notes?'

'No! What was that?'

'I wish I could have been there . . . At the Bougival weir . . . Two mornings ago . . . Thousand-franc notes floating on the tide . . . It was a sailor who spotted them first and who managed to fish out a few . . . but the lock-keeper saw what was going on and called the police and an officer kept an eye out for anyone trying going after the loot.'

'No kidding? I don't suppose that stopped them putting a bit aside.'

'The paper says they found around thirty notes, but that there must have been a lot more, because they fished out a couple down river in Mantes too . . . Huh! Cash swimming down the Seine! It's better than gudgeon.'

Maigret stood a head taller than everyone else. He remained impassive, his face composed.

. . . because he didn't bring home the money.

So was that it? Meek Monsieur Martin, overcome by fear or remorse at the thought of his crime? Martin who admitted he went for a walk that evening on the Ile Saint-Louis to relieve his neuralgia!

Maigret couldn't help smiling a little as he pictured Madame Martin, who had seen it all from her window and was waiting.

Her husband came home, weary, defeated. She watched his every action and movement. She was eager to see the notes, perhaps to count them.

He got undressed and prepared for bed.

Didn't she pick up his clothes to search his pockets?

She started to feel anxious. She looked at Martin with his droopy moustache.

'The . . . the . . . money?'

'What money?'

'Who did you give it to? Answer me! Don't try and lie.'

And Maigret, alighting from the omnibus at Pont-Neuf, from where he could see the windows of his office, caught himself saying in a low voice, 'I bet once he was in bed, Martin began to cry!'

10. *Identity Cards*

It began at Jeumont. The time was eleven p.m. A few third-class passengers walked towards the customs shed while the customs officers began inspecting the second- and first-class carriages.

Meticulous people had got their suitcases down in advance and spread the contents out on the seats. This included a man with anxious eyes in second class, in a compartment where the only other passengers were an elderly Belgian couple.

His luggage was a model of neatness and forethought. His shirts were wrapped in newspaper to prevent them getting dirty. There were twelve pairs of detachable cuffs, winter drawers and summer drawers, an alarm clock, shoes and a pair of worn-out slippers.

A woman's hand had clearly done the packing. There was no wasted space. Nothing would get creased. A customs officer poked around carelessly, observing the man in the putty-coloured overcoat, who looked just the type to have such suitcases.

'All right!'

A chalk cross on the cases.

'Anything to declare, the rest of you?'

'Excuse me,' asked the man, 'where exactly does Belgium begin?'

'You see the first hedge over there? No! You can't see anything! But look . . . Count the lamps . . . the third on the left . . . Well, that's the border.'

A voice in the corridor, repeating at the door of each compartment, 'Have your passports ready, your identity cards!'

And the man in the putty-coloured overcoat struggled to put his suitcases back in the overhead net.

'Passport?'

He turned around and saw a young man wearing a grey peaked cap.

'French? Your identity card, then.'

It took a few moments. His fingers rummaged in his wallet.

'Here you are, monsieur!'

'Good! Martin, Edgar Émile . . . That's correct! . . . Follow me—'

'Where to?'

'You can bring your luggage.'

'But . . . the train—'

The two Belgians now stared at him, aghast, although they were amused to have shared a compartment with a fugitive. Monsieur Martin, his eyes wide, clambered up on to the seat to retrieve his suitcases.

'I swear . . . What the—?'

'Hurry up . . . The train's about to leave.'

And the young man in the grey cap rolled the heaviest suitcase on to the platform. It was dark. In the glow of the lamplight, people were hurrying back from the buffet. The whistle was blown. A woman was arguing with the customs officers who refused to allow her back on to the train.

'We'll see about that in the morning—'

And Monsieur Martin followed the young man, struggling to carry his suitcases. He had never thought a station platform could be so long. It went on and on, endless, deserted, with mysterious doors leading off it.

Finally, they went through the last one.

'Come in!'

It was dark. Nothing but a lamp with a green shade, hanging so low above the table that it only shed light on a few papers. And yet something was moving at the far end of the room.

'Good evening, Monsieur Martin,' said a cordial voice.

And a burly form stepped out of the shadows: Detective Chief Inspector Maigret, encased in his heavy overcoat with a velvet collar, his hands in his pockets.

'Don't bother taking off your coat. We're getting the train back to Paris, which is due to arrive on platform three.'

This time it was definite! Martin was crying, silently, his hands paralysed by his neatly packed suitcases.

The inspector who had been placed on sentry duty at 61, Place des Vosges had telephoned Maigret a few hours earlier, 'Our man is running off. He's just taken a taxi to the Gare du Nord.'

'Let him get away. Carry on watching the wife.'

And Maigret had caught the same train as Martin. He had travelled in the neighbouring compartment with two sergeants who had told lewd stories for the entire duration of the journey.

From time to time, the chief inspector peeped through the spy hole between the two compartments and glimpsed a gloomy Martin.

Jeumont . . . Identity card! . . . Border police.

Now, they were both on their way back to Paris, in a reserved compartment. Martin was not handcuffed. His suitcases were in the net above his head, and one of them, precariously balanced, threatened to fall on him.

They had reached Maubeuge and Maigret still hadn't asked a single question.

It was unbelievable! He was ensconced in his corner, his pipe between his teeth. He puffed away continually, watching his companion with his laughing little eyes.

Ten times, twenty times, Martin opened his mouth without saying anything. Ten times, twenty times, the chief inspector took absolutely no notice.

And eventually it happened: an indescribable voice, which Madame Martin herself would probably not have recognized.

'It's me—'

And Maigret still didn't say a word. His pupils seemed to say, 'Really?'

'I . . . I was hoping to make it across the border—'

There is a way of smoking that is aggravating for the person watching the smoker: with each puff, his lips part sensuously, making a little 'puk' sound. And the smoke isn't puffed out in front, but escapes slowly and forms a cloud around his face.

Maigret smoked like this and his head nodded from right to left and left to right to the rhythm of the train.

Martin leaned forward, his hands hurting inside his gloves, his eyes feverish.

'Do you think it'll be long? . . . It won't, will it? Because I confess . . . I confess everything—'

How did he manage to hold back his sobs? His nerves must have been utterly frayed. And his eyes, from time to time, were beseeching Maigret: 'Please help me! . . . You can see that I have no strength left.'

But the chief inspector did not budge. He was as calm, with the same curious, detached gaze as if he were in front of an exotic animal's cage at the zoological gardens.

'Couchet caught me . . . So—'

And Maigret sighed. A sigh that meant nothing, or rather that could be interpreted in a hundred different ways.

Saint-Quentin! Footsteps in the corridor. A portly passenger tried to open the door of the compartment, realized it was locked, stood there for a moment looking in, his nose pressed to the pane, and then finally resigned himself to looking for another seat.

'Because I confess everything, you see? There's no point denying—'

Exactly as if he had spoken to a deaf man, or to a man who did not understand a wretched word of French. Maigret filled his pipe, meticulously tapping it with his index finger.

'Do you have any matches?'

'No . . . I don't smoke, as you know very well. My wife doesn't like the smell of tobacco. I want it to be done quickly, do you understand? I'll say so to the lawyer that I'll have to choose. No complications! I confess everything. I read in the paper that some of the money's been found. I don't know why I did that. I could feel it in my pocket and I had the impression that everyone in the street was looking at me. At first I thought of hiding it somewhere, but to do what with it?

'I walked along the embankment. There were barges. I was afraid of being seen by a bargeman. So I crossed the Pont-Marie and was able to get rid of the bundle on the Ile Saint-Louis.'

The compartment was boiling hot; condensation ran down the windows, pipe smoke curled around the lamp.

'I should have confessed everything to you the first time I saw you. I didn't have the courage. I hoped that—'

Martin fell silent and stared curiously at his companion, who had half-opened his mouth and closed his eyes. His breathing was regular like the purring of a fat, satiated cat.

Maigret was asleep!

Martin glanced over at the door, which only needed a push. And, as if to avoid the temptation, he huddled in a corner, clenching his buttocks, his twitching hands resting on his scrawny knees.

Gare du Nord. A grey morning. And the herd of commuters, still drowsy, streaming out.

The train had stopped a long way from the concourse. The suitcases were heavy. Martin didn't want to stop. He was out of breath and his arms hurt.

They had to wait a long time for a taxi.

'Are you taking me to prison?'

They had spent five hours on trains and Maigret hadn't uttered ten sentences. If that! Words that had nothing to do either with the murder or with the 360,000 francs. He had talked about his pipe, or the heat, or the arrival time.

'Sixty-one, Place des Vosges!' he instructed the driver.

Martin implored him, 'Do you think it's necessary to—?'

And to himself, 'What must they be thinking at the office! There wasn't time to let them know—'

The concierge was in her lodge, sorting out the post: a huge pile of letters for Doctor Rivière's Serums. A tiny pile for the rest of the residents.

'Monsieur Martin! Monsieur Martin! Someone came from the Registry Office to see if you were ill . . . Apparently you've got the key to—'

Maigret dragged his companion away. And Martin had to lug his heavy suitcases up the stairs. There were milk cans and fresh bread outside the apartment doors.

Old Mathilde's door moved.

'Give me the key.'

'But—'

'Open it yourself.'

A profound silence. The click of the lock. Then they saw the tidy dining room, every object in its rightful place.

Martin hesitated for a long time before saying out loud, 'It's me! . . . And the detective chief inspector—'

Someone moved in the bed in the adjacent bedroom. Martin closed the door behind them and groaned, 'We shouldn't have . . . She's not in any way to blame, is she? And in her condition—'

He didn't dare enter the bedroom. To maintain his composure, he picked up his suitcases and placed them on two chairs.

'Shall I make some coffee?'

Maigret knocked on the bedroom door.

'May I come in?'

No reply. He pushed open the door and received the full force of Madame Martin's stare. She was in bed, motionless, curling pins in her hair.

'I'm sorry to disturb you . . . I've brought home your husband, who made the mistake of panicking.'

Martin was behind him. He could sense him, but he couldn't see him.

Footsteps could be heard in the courtyard, and voices, chiefly women's voices: the office and laboratory staff arriving. It was one minute to nine.

A muffled cry from the madwoman next door. Medication on the bedside table.

'Are you feeling worse?'

He knew very well that she wouldn't answer, that despite everything, she would maintain the same staunch reserve.

She seemed afraid of saying a word, a single one. As if one word could unleash disaster!

She had grown thinner and her complexion had become duller. But her eyes, on the other hand, those strange grey pupils, had a fiery, wilful life of their own.

Martin entered, his legs weak. His entire demeanour was apologetic, as if asking for forgiveness.

The icy grey eyes swivelled slowly to look at him, so piercingly that he looked away, stammering, 'It was at Jeumont station . . . One more minute and I'd have been in Belgium.'

Words, sentences, noise were needed, to fill the void that could be sensed around each individual. A void that was tangible, to the point that voices echoed as in a tunnel or a cave.

But no one spoke. They struggled to articulate a few syllables, with anxious glances, then silence fell in the implacable manner of a fog.

And yet something was happening. Something slow, insidious: a hand slid beneath the blanket and in an imperceptible movement inched its way up to the pillow.

Madame Martin's thin, clammy hand. Maigret, while looking elsewhere, followed its progress, waiting for the moment when that hand would finally reach its goal.

'Isn't the doctor supposed to be coming this morning?'

'I don't know . . . Is anyone looking after me? I'm lying here like an animal left to die.'

But her eyes became brighter because her hand finally touched the object she was seeking.

A barely audible rustle of paper.

Maigret took a step forward and seized Madame Martin's wrist. She seemed to have no strength, almost no life. Even so, from one moment to the next, she displayed an unimaginable vigour.

She refused to let go of whatever she was holding. Sitting up in bed, she fought back furiously. She raised her hand to her mouth. With her teeth she tore the sheet of white paper she was clutching.

'Let me go! Let me go or I'll scream! . . . And you? Are you just going to stand there?'

'Detective Chief Inspector . . . I beg you,' groaned Martin.

He was listening out. He was afraid the residents would come running. He didn't dare step in.

'Beast! Filthy beast! Hitting a woman!'

No, Maigret wasn't hitting her. He simply held her wrist in his grip, squeezing a little hard perhaps, to stop the woman from destroying the document.

'Aren't you ashamed! A dying woman—'

A woman who displayed an energy the like of which Maigret had rarely encountered in his career in the police! His bowler hat fell on to the bed. She suddenly bit the inspector's wrist.

But she could not keep her nerves so tensed for long, and he managed to prise her fingers open; she gave a howl of pain.

Now she was crying, crying without tears, crying out of vexation, out of rage, perhaps also to strike a pose?

'And you just stood there and let him—'

Maigret's back was too broad for the narrow bedroom. He seemed to fill the entire space, blocking out the light.

He went over to the fireplace, smoothed out the sheet of paper with bits missing, and ran his eyes over a typed text on letterhead paper.

Laval and Piollet
of the Paris bar
Counsels in chambers
Solicitors

On the right, in red: *Re Couchet vs. Martin. Advice of 18 November.*

Two pages of dense, single-spaced typing. Maigret only read fragments, in a quiet voice, while typewriters could be heard clattering in the offices of Doctor Rivière's Serums.

In view of the law of . . .

Given that Roger Couchet's death occurred subsequent to that of his father . . .

. . . that no will can deprive a legitimate son of his rightful share . . .

. . . that the second marriage of the testator to Madame Dormoy was under the joint estate system . . .

. . . that Roger Couchet's natural heir is his mother . . .

. . . have the honour of confirming that you are entitled to claim half of Raymond Couchet's estate, including both movable and immovable assets . . . which, according to the specific informa-

*tion we have received and subject to adjustment for errors or
omissions, we value at around five million, the establishment
known as 'Doctor Rivière's Serums' itself being estimated at
three million . . .*

*. . . We remain at your service to take any steps necessary to
nullify the will and . . .*

*Confirm that of the sums recovered we will retain a commission
of ten per cent (10%) for costs . . .*

Madame Martin had stopped crying. She was lying down
again and her frosty gaze was once more directed at the
ceiling.

Martin stood in the doorway, more disconcerted than
ever, not knowing what to do with his hands, his eyes, his
entire body.

'There's a postscript!' muttered Maigret to himself.

The postscript was preceded by the words: *Strictly con-
fidential.*

*It is our belief that Madame Couchet, née Dormoy, is also
minded to contest the will.*

*Furthermore, we have made enquiries about the third benefi-
ciary, Nine Moinard. She is a woman of dubious reputation,
who has not yet taken any steps to claim her due.*

*Given that she is currently without any resources, it seems to
us that the most expeditious solution would be to offer her a
sum of money as compensation.*

We would suggest the sum of twenty thousand francs, which is likely to delight a person in Mlle Moinard's situation.

We await your decision on this matter.

Maigret had allowed his pipe to go out. He slowly folded the document and slipped it into his wallet.

Around him, all was absolute silence. Martin seemed to be holding his breath. His wife, on the bed, staring fixedly, already looked like a corpse.

'Two million, five hundred thousand francs,' murmured the chief inspector. 'Minus the twenty thousand francs to be given to Nine to ensure she would be accommodating . . . It's true that Madame Couchet will probably contribute half—'

He was certain that a triumphant smile, faint but eloquent, hovered on the woman's lips.

'That's a hefty sum! . . . I say, Martin—'

Martin gave a start, tried to put himself on the defensive.

'What do you expect to receive? . . . I'm not talking about money . . . I'm talking about your sentence . . . Theft . . . Murder . . . Perhaps they'll establish that there was premeditation . . . In your opinion? . . . No acquittal, naturally, since it wasn't a crime of passion . . . Oh! If only your wife had resumed relations with her former husband . . . but that is not the case . . . A question of money, purely of money . . . Ten years? . . . Twenty years? . . . Do you want to know what I think? . . . Mind you, it's never possible to guess at the decisions of jurors . . . Although there have been precedents . . . Well, we can say that in general, while they tend to be lenient when it comes to crimes of passion, they are extremely harsh in cases involving personal gain . . .'

It was as if he were talking for the sake of talking, playing for time.

'That's understandable! They are petty bourgeois, traders . . . They believe they have nothing to fear from mistresses they don't have or who they trust . . . but they have a lot to fear from thieves . . . Twenty years? . . . Well, no! . . . I reckon it'll be the guillotine—'

Martin didn't budge. He was now even more ashen-faced than his wife. He had to hold on to the door frame for support.

'Except that Madame Martin will be rich . . . She's at the age when a person knows how to enjoy life and wealth—'

He walked over to the window.

'Unless this window . . . This is the stumbling block . . . It is bound to be pointed out that everything could be seen from here . . . Everything, you hear! And that is serious! . . . Because that would make her an accessory . . . And in fact, the criminal code states that accessories to a murder are prohibited from being beneficiaries of the victim's will. It's not only the murderer, but the accomplices too . . . You see now how important this window is—'

It was no longer silence that was surrounding him, it was something more absolute, more worrying, almost unreal: a total absence of any life.

And suddenly, a question, 'Tell me, Martin! What did you do with the gun?'

A rustle in the corridor: old Mathilde, of course, with her moon face and her soft belly under her gingham apron.

The concierge's shrill voice in the courtyard.

'Madame Martin! . . . It's the Dufayel man!'

Maigret sat in a wing chair that wobbled but didn't break straight away.

11. *The Drawing on the Wall*

'Answer me! The gun—'

He followed Martin's gaze and noticed that Madame Martin, who was still staring at the ceiling, was moving her fingers against the wall.

Poor Martin was making desperate efforts to understand what she meant. He grew impatient. He could see that Maigret was waiting.

'I—'

What could that square or trapeze that she was outlining with her thin finger mean?

'Well?'

At that moment, Maigret truly pitied him. This must be terrible for him. Martin was gasping with impatience.

'I threw it in the Seine.'

The die was cast! As the chief inspector pulled the gun out of his pocket and placed it on the table, Madame Martin sat up in bed, fuming.

'I did eventually find it in the dustbin,' said Maigret.

And then the feverish woman hissed, 'There! Do you understand now? Are you happy? You missed your chance, once again, as you always have done! Anyone would think you did it on purpose, for fear of going to prison . . . but you'll go to prison anyway! Because you were the thief! The 360 notes that monsieur threw into the Seine—'

She was terrifying. It was clear that she had bottled everything up inside her for too long. The release was violent. And she was so carried away that sometimes several words reached her lips at the same time and tumbled over each other.

Martin bowed his head. His part was over. As his wife said, he had failed miserably.

'. . . Monsieur takes it into his head to steal, but he leaves his glove on the table—'

All Madame Martin's resentment was going to burst out, messily, chaotically.

Behind him Maigret heard the voice of the man with the putty-coloured overcoat.

'For months she'd been pointing at the office to me through the window, Couchet, who was always going to the toilet . . . and she rebuked me for making her so miserable, for being incapable of feeding a wife . . . I went down there—'

'Did you tell her that you were going?'

'No! But she knew. She was at the window.'

'And from a distance you saw the glove that your husband had left behind, Madame Martin?'

'As if he were leaving a calling card! Anyone would think he did it on purpose to annoy me—'

'You picked up your gun and you went there . . . Couchet returned while you were in the office . . . He thought it was you who had stolen—'

'He wanted to have me arrested! That's what he wanted to do! As if it weren't thanks to me that he'd become rich! . . . Who'd looked after him, in the early days, when he barely earned enough to eat bread without any butter? . . . All men are the same! . . . He even reprimanded me for living in the building where he had his offices. He accused me of sharing the money he gave my son.'

'And you shot him?'

'He had already picked up the telephone to call the police!'

'You headed for the dustbins. Saying you were looking for a silver spoon, you hid the gun in the rubbish. Who did you bump into then?'

She spat, 'That stupid old man from the first floor.'

'Nobody else? I thought your son came by. He was out of money.'

'So what?'

'He hadn't come to see you, but his father, isn't that right? Only you couldn't allow him to go into the office, where he would have discovered the body. You were both in the courtyard. What did you say to Roger?'

'I told him to go away. You can't understand a mother's heart.'

'And he left. Your husband came home. Neither of you mentioned anything . . . Is that right? . . . Martin was thinking of the notes he'd ended up throwing into the Seine, because deep down he's a poor devil of a good man.'

'Poor devil of a good man!' echoed Madame Martin with an unexpected fury. 'Ha! Ha! And what about me? I've always been unhappy—'

'Martin doesn't know who has killed . . . He goes to bed. A day goes by without you saying anything . . . But the following night you get up to search the clothes he's taken off . . . You look for the money in vain . . . He watches you . . . You question him . . . And it's the outburst of anger that old Mathilde overheard behind the door . . . You've killed for nothing! That idiot Martin has thrown the money away! He has thrown a fortune in the Seine, for lack of guts! It makes you ill . . . You go down with a fever . . . And Martin, who is unaware that you are the killer, goes and tells Roger the news. And Roger realizes the truth. He saw you in the courtyard . . . You stopped him from going into the office. He knows you. He thinks I suspect him. He imagines that he'll be arrested, accused . . . and he can't defend himself without accusing his mother . . . Perhaps he's not a very nice boy . . . But there are probably good reasons why he ended up living as he did. He's full of loathing . . . loathing for the women he sleeps with, loathing for the drugs, for Montmartre where he hangs around, and, above all, for this family tragedy in which he alone is aware of all the motives. He jumps out of the window!'

Martin was leaning against the wall, his face buried in his folded arms. But his wife gazed fixedly at the inspector, as if she were just waiting for the right time to interrupt his account, and attack him back.

Then Maigret produced the lawyers' written advice.

'During my last visit, Martin was so panic-stricken that he was about to confess his theft . . . but you were there . . . He could see you through the doorway . . . You frantically signalled to him and he held his tongue. Is that not what finally opened his eyes? He questioned you. Yes, you had killed! You screamed in his face! You killed because of him, to make up for his mistake, because of that glove left on the desk! And, because you have killed, you won't even inherit, despite the will! Oh! If only Martin were a man! Let him go abroad. People will believe he's guilty. The police will go away and you'll go and join him with the millions. Poor old Martin!'

And Maigret almost crushed the man with a formidable clap on the shoulder. He spoke in a muted voice. He let the words fall without insisting.

'To have done all that for the money! Couchet's death, Roger throwing himself out of the window, and then to realize at the last minute that you won't get it! You'd rather pack Martin's bags yourself. Neatly arranged suitcases. Months' worth of underwear—'

'Stop!' begged Martin.

The madwoman screamed. Maigret flung open the door and old Mathilde almost tumbled into the room!

She fled, terrified at the inspector's tone of voice, and for the first time she shut her door properly and turned the key in the lock.

Maigret glanced around the room one last time. Martin didn't dare move. His thin wife sitting up in bed, her shoulder blades prominent beneath her nightshirt, followed the police officer with her eyes.

She was so serious, so calm all of a sudden, that Maigret wondered, anxiously, what she had up her sleeve.

He remembered certain looks, during the earlier scene, certain movements of her lips. And he intuited, at exactly the same time as Martin, what was happening.

There were unable to stop her. The whole thing happened independently of them, like a nightmare.

Madame Martin was very, very thin. And her features became even more tormented. What was she staring at, in places where there was nothing but the usual bedroom objects?

What was she watching attentively moving around the room?

Her forehead furrowed. Her temples throbbed. Martin cried, 'I'm scared!'

Nothing had changed in the apartment. A lorry drove into the courtyard and they could hear the concierge's shrill voice.

It was as though Madame Martin was making a huge effort, all alone, to scale an impossible mountain. Twice her hand made a movement as if to swat something away from her face. Finally, she swallowed her saliva and smiled like someone who has reached their goal, 'All the same, you'll all come and ask me for money. I'm going to tell my lawyer not to give you any.'

Martin was twitching from head to toe. He realized that this was no passing delirium caused by her fever.

She had lost her mind, permanently!

'You can't blame her. She's never been like everyone else, has she?' he moaned.

He was awaiting the inspector's confirmation.

'Poor Martin—'

Martin was crying! He seized his wife's hand and was rubbing his face against it. She pushed him away. She had a superior, contemptuous smile.

'No more than five francs at a time. I've suffered enough, I have, of—'

'I'm going to call Sainte-Anne's' said Maigret.

'Do you think? Does she . . . does she need to be locked up?'

Force of habit? Martin was panic-stricken at the idea of leaving his home, that atmosphere of resentment and daily quarrels, that sordid life, that wife who, one last time, was trying to think but who, disconsolate and defeated, lay back with a great sigh, stammering, 'Bring me the key—'

A few moments later, Maigret crossed the teeming street like a stranger. He had a throbbing headache, something that occurred rarely, and he went into a pharmacy to buy a pill.

He couldn't see anything around him. The sounds of the city blended with others, with voices in particular, which continued to resonate in his head.

One image in particular haunted him: Madame Martin getting up, picking her husband's clothes up from the floor and looking for the money. And Martin watching her from the bed.

The woman's questioning gaze!

'I threw it into the Seine.'

It was at that moment that something had snapped. Or rather there had always been something not right in her brain! It was already so when she lived in the confectioner's at Meaux.

Only it wasn't noticeable. She was an almost-pretty girl. No one worried about her too-thin lips.

And Couchet had married her!

'What would become of me if something happened to you?'

Maigret had to wait to cross the Boulevard Beaumarchais. For no reason, Nine came into his mind.

'She'll get nothing, not a *sou,*' he murmured. 'The family will have the will revoked. And it is Madame Couchet, née Dormoy—'

The colonel must have begun the formalities. It was natural. Madame Couchet would get everything. All those millions—'

She was a distinguished woman, who would maintain her station.

Maigret slowly climbed the stairs and pushed open the door of the apartment in Boulevard Richard-Lenoir.

'Guess what happened?'

Madame Maigret was setting four places on the white tablecloth. Maigret noticed a small jug of plum brandy on the sideboard.

'Your sister!'

It wasn't difficult to guess, because each time she came from Alsace, she brought fruit brandy and a smoked ham.

'She's gone to buy some things with André.'

The husband. A good fellow who managed a brickworks.

'You look tired. I hope you're not going out again today at least?'

Maigret did not go out. At nine p.m., he was playing Pope Joan with his sister and brother-in-law. The dining room was fragrant with the smell of plum brandy.

And Madame Maigret kept giggling because she'd never

understood cards and she made every silly mistake imaginable.

'Are you sure you haven't got a nine?'

'No, I've got one—'

'So why don't you put it down?'

For Maigret, all that had the soothing effect of a hot bath. His headache was gone.

He no longer thought about Madame Martin, who had been taken by ambulance to Sainte-Anne's, while her husband sobbed alone in the empty stairwell.

THE GRAND BANKS CAFÉ

GEORGES SIMENON

It was indeed a photo, a picture of a woman. But the face was completely hidden, scribbled all over in red ink. Someone had tried to obliterate the head, someone very angry. The pen had bitten into the paper. There were so many criss-crossed lines that not a single square millimetre had been left visible.

Captain Fallut's last voyage is shrouded in silence. To discover the truth about this doomed expedition, Maigret enters a remote, murky world of men on the margins of society; where fierce loyalties hide sordid affairs.

Translated by David Coward

OTHER TITLES IN THE SERIES

MAN'S HEAD
EORGES SIMENON

*e stared at Maigret, who stared back and found no trace of
unkenness in his companion's face.*

*stead he saw the same eyes ablaze with acute intelligence which
ere now fixed on him with a look of consummate irony, as though
adek were truly possessed by fierce exultant joy.*

n audacious plan to prove the innocence of a young drifter
vaiting execution takes Maigret through the grey, autumnal streets
Paris. As he pursues the true culprit from lonely docks to elegant
tels and fashionable bars, he confronts the destructive power of a
ngerously sharp intellect.

anslated by David Coward

OTHER TITLES IN THE SERIES

THE DANCER AT THE GAI-MOULIN
GEORGES SIMENON

They could not exactly hear the music. They could guess at it. What could be sensed above all was the beat from the drummer. A rhythm throbbing through the air and bringing back the image of the club's interior with its crimson velvet seats, the tinkle of glasses and the woman in pink dancing with a man in a tuxedo.

Maigret observes from a distance as two teenage boys are accused of killing a rich foreigner in a seedy club in Liège. As the disturbing truth about the man's death emerges, greed, pride and envy start to drive the two friends apart.

Translated by Siân Reynolds

NSPECTOR MAIGRET

OTHER TITLES IN THE SERIES

THE TWO-PENNY BAR
GEORGES SIMENON

A radiant late afternoon. The sunshine almost as thick as syrup in the quiet streets of the Left Bank . . . there are days like this, when ordinary life seems heightened, when the people walking down the street, the trams and cars all seem to exist in a fairy tale.

A story told by a condemned man leads Maigret to a bar by the Seine and into the sleazy underside of respectable Parisian life. In the oppressive heat of summer, a forgotten crime comes to life.

Translated by David Watson

Previously published as *The Bar on the Seine*

OTHER TITLES IN THE SERIES

And more to follow